Reckless

SHATTERED SISTERS #1

MAGGIE SHAYNE

THUNDERFOOT PUBLISHING, INC.

Dear Reader,

The story you are about to read was the very first one I ever published. Now, some ninety titles later, this story and these characters remain as key players in one of the most memorable days of my life.

Picture it: small-town U.S.A. in the summer of 1992. A harried young mother of five little girls with a dream—a dream she's been steadfastly pursuing for more than five years. I didn't work outside the home then—I had vowed that I'd get an outside job when my youngest daughter started kindergarten, and that time was drawing very near. As August wore on and September drew near, I began looking at the want ads.

Then came August 24. I returned home from grocery shopping to find a message waiting. An editor, who said she would call me back later. I was almost afraid to hope, but she did call back and all the girls crowded around me, listening. They'd been with me on this journey for more than five years. They understood how hard I had tried, how many times I had been rejected and gone to bed crying, only to drag myself back to the typewriter to try again. Yes, typewriter. I didn't have a computer. I had taken care of a neighbor's horse farm for a long weekend to earn the money to go from a manual typewriter to an electric one, and even that was a big expense back then. I thought corrector ribbon was the greatest invention of all time. (I had not yet discovered the internet.)

My girls knew what it meant when that editor told me that one of the stories I had written was going to be published. And when I put the phone down, you never heard so much shrieking, squealing, and laughter in your life.

This book, this very story, was the turning point from struggling, aspiring author, writing stuff that was "close but not quite right," to professional author living a lifelong dream. *Reckless Angel* was the key that unlocked the door to my future. It's as precious to me as a part of my family.

I have gone back through this story and rewritten it extensively. I'm a better writer than I was back then, and times have changed. In the original, the heroine didn't even have a cell phone.

I think the story is worthy of standing beside my more recent works, and I truly hope you enjoy it!

Best always,
Maggie Shayne

The Shattered Sisters Series

CHAPTER 1

In the murky, rain-veiled light that spilled into a
filthy alley, Nick watched the gruesome scene play
out. The man who called himself *Viper* leaned over
his victim's body, his face alternately beige and bright
orange in the flickering light of a broken neon sign.
He grunted as he pulled his bloody blade from the
dead man's chest. Nick turned up his collar when the
rain came down colder and harder than before. He
was glad of the rain. There would be less blood.

Something moved and Nick gave a quick glance
up the alley, simultaneously lifting his 9 mm semi-
automatic. The gun's muzzle moved in perfect
unison with his eyes until he found the source of the
sound in an overflowing trash bin. Just a rat. Red eyes
glowed in a shiny black coat for an instant before it
scurried away, and Nick resumed watching the little
man with the pinched face and the intimidating
nickname. Truth was, the hitman looked more like a

weasel than a snake.

"Boss doesn't want Vinnie ID'ed right away," Nick reminded him.

Viper shook his head, but his slicked-back hair didn't move. "I've done my part." He wiped the blade over the dead man's lapel and started to stand.

Nick worked the action of the gun, chambering a round to make his point, and Viper's head snapped toward him.

"Lou sent me to witness the hit, not clean up after it. You don't want to do it, either—that's fine with me. Just let me come along when you tell Lou why Vinnie was ID'ed before he was stiff." He knew his voice was like cold steel. He wanted it that way. He pretended great interest in the blue-black barrel of his gun while Viper, who'd been working for Lou a lot longer than Nick had, and resented being assigned a babysitter, made up his mind.

After a long moment Viper knelt again to begin removing items from his victim's pockets. He took the ring from his finger, ripped the tags out of his clothes. He handed those items to Nick and bent once more, this time intent on rubbing the corpse's fingertips back and forth over rough pavement until no trace of a print remained. Nick stuffed the victim's belongings into a plastic zipper bag and pushed it into the pocket of his raincoat.

Then Viper pulled a small-caliber revolver from his own coat, held it two inches from the dead face and thumbed the hammer back.

A sound like a gag made them both swing their

heads toward the sidewalk where a woman stood, frozen, staring into the alley. Nick's gaze locked with hers. She stared right back at him, and there was no doubt in his mind that she was memorizing his every feature, better to describe him to the local cops she intended to call. Viper lifted his gun her way.

Nick swung one arm downward, knocking Viper's muzzle off target before the other man had a chance to pull the trigger. "Finish *this* job, dammit. I'll take care of her." She was already off and running, so Nick sprinted for the opposite end of the alley. She would head around the block—to the closest place with lights and people. He vaulted the mesh fence that blocked the alley at the back end and landed with a jarring thud on the pavement. Then he moved silently, keeping close to the buildings.

He stopped when he heard her heels smacking rapidly over the wet sidewalk, waited to step into her path when she came around the corner at breakneck speed, cellphone in hand, looking down at its screen instead of up where she was going.

She careened into his chest and the phone clattered to the ground. He felt the heat emanating from her, heard her ragged breathing. "Thank God," she said on a noisy exhale. "I need—" She looked up into his eyes and she knew.

Before she could pull back, he clamped his hands on her shoulders. When her full lips parted, Nick said, "Scream and you die, lady." She didn't. She pressed her lips tight and swallowed hard. Nick saw her fear. He felt it. It surrounded her like a halo of light around a candle's flame. He watched her, ready to react to her slightest move.

Wild black curls hung past her shoulders and glittered with clinging raindrops reflecting the city lights. Her eyes—they looked black, too, but he couldn't be sure in the darkness—were wide with fear, but alert and intelligent. She was small, so she wouldn't be hard to handle. The top of her head didn't quite reach his chin.

He heard footsteps in the distance, half trot, half shuffle—Viper's unmistakable gait, coming around the block the same way the woman had. If Nick didn't think of something fast, the little bastard would probably put them both on ice. He held the gun under her nose, so she could get a good look. She refused to glance down. She stared up at him instead, her eyes still afraid but defiant. He could see the wheels turning behind those eyes. It surprised him to realize that he knew what she was thinking. She was weighing the odds, waiting for a chance. She'd knee him in the balls or try some half-assed move she'd learned in a self-defense class and run like hell if he gave her an opening. And then she'd end up dead.

"Listen and listen good." Nick used his best street voice and most intimidating tone. "The guy you hear coming is a killer—a pro. When he gets here, he's gonna make you his next job, then he's gonna do the same for me 'cause I didn't off you myself. You got one chance. You wanna see tomorrow, you do what I say, *to the letter*. You got it?"

She didn't acknowledge the question in the slightest, but just kept watching him with those unbelievably huge, liquid eyes. He blinked and made himself continue. "When I let go of you, run past me, same way you were heading. I'm gonna fire one shot, and you're gonna hit the pavement and play dead for all you're worth."

Viper's footsteps drew nearer. The woman's gaze flicked away from his to glance back over her shoulder. She looked up at him again, a little of the defiance gone. "What if I don't?" The words sounded as if they were forced through a space too small for them.

"If you don't, lady, then the second shot will be for real. And I never miss." He let the words fall heavily between them, saw her go a shade paler. She glanced down at her cell phone, lying on the sidewalk at her feet. He did too, and then he stomped on it. "It's me or him, lady. Only difference is, he'll kill you." He looked up again, waited for her to meet his eyes, and added. "I won't."

After a drawn-out second, she nodded.

Nick drew a steadying breath, released her shoulders and stepped aside to let her go by him. "Go."

She ran. Nick picked up the cell phone, just in case, pocketed it, and waited for Viper to come around the corner so he'd have a good view, then raised the gun, aiming over the woman's head and squeezed the trigger. He never realized he'd been holding his breath until she went down and he released it all at once. She lay still, facedown on the sidewalk some forty feet away. Viper reached him a second later.

"You get her?"

Lights came on in apartment windows. Nick had no doubt that someone was dialing 911. "You got eyes?"

Viper looked toward the girl and started forward. "Damn, that broad looked familiar."

"What did you do with Vinnie?" Nick's barked question stopped the other man in his tracks.

"In my trunk."

"Get him the hell outta here. Place'll be crawling with cops any minute."

Viper looked toward her again, and Nick saw the doubt in his eyes. He needed more convincing. Nick dug into his pocket for his keys and tossed them to the smaller man. "My car's around the corner. Get it over here before you take off."

"What do I look like, a damn parking attendant?"

A head poked out of a second story window, then ducked back inside. The window closed with a bang. Viper muttered a curse and dashed back around the corner, moving unevenly but quickly. Nick went to the fallen woman, leaning close, whispering near her ear, he said, "Good job. Now play along. He's got to believe this is real. Our lives are on the line."

She didn't respond.

Nick's car came to a screeching halt at the curb. He rolled her onto her back, and she went like a wet rag. Perfectly limp. She was putting on one hell of a show. He grabbed her under the arms and pulled her up and over his shoulder, and wrapping one arm firmly around her thighs to hold her there, took three steps to the car.

Her hands dangled loosely against his back. Her legs felt cold beneath his hand. Stupid woman, he thought, walking around in a skirt on a night like this. "Pop the trunk, Viper." His thumb inadvertently rubbed her bare thigh and his mouth went dry.

He dumped her unceremoniously inside, hard enough so Viper could feel the car sink with her weight, then slammed the trunk hard and went to the driver's door. Viper got out of the car, and Nick slid behind the wheel. "Where you dumpin' Vinnie?" he asked.

"East River," Viper answered quickly. He was nervous now, looking around. A faint siren came wailing from somewhere, and his eyes danced in their sockets.

"I'll take her somewhere else then. We don't want any connections," Nick said. "Let's go."

Viper nodded and hurried into the darkness like a cockroach when the lights come on. A second later, Nick spun his black Lincoln around and took off.

He managed to avoid the police, taking side streets until he was sure he hadn't been followed. He managed to take the battery out of the phone and toss it out the window as he drove. Then he pulled to the curb on an empty street, between a crumbling, condemned heap and a weedy vacant lot. Most of the streetlights had been shot out or demolished with stones. Getting out, hunching against the rain, he went to the back of the car and thumbed the trunk release on his keyring.

The rain fell harder. He tightened the belt of his raincoat and leaned inside. The only light was the tiny bulb that came on whenever the trunk was opened. "Come on out," he said softly, glancing around once more to be sure he wasn't being watched. She didn't move. He leaned lower, frowning. "Lady, you can cut the act now." He pushed at her shoulder with one hand, but she remained as she was, a small, wet, unmoving bundle. Nick's blood slowed to a stop in his veins. Could he possibly have—

"Oh, *hell*, no." He gripped her shoulders and shook her a little. When she still didn't respond, he pushed the damp, tangled masses of hair away from her face in search of an exit wound or a trace of blood. He'd aimed high. If he'd hit her it would be a headshot. Hell. He bent close to her, so close he could smell her perfume. It wrapped around his mind and tugged. He saw the tiny beads of rain clinging to her face.

When her feet suddenly slammed into his solar plexus it was like an explosion. He stumbled backward, pain shooting in every direction, and doubled over, struggling to draw a breath and failing. When he finally blinked enough moisture from his eyes to see straight and managed to unbend himself and actually inhale, he glimpsed her running like hell in the direction they'd come from. Swearing under his breath, he dove back into the car, pulled it around in a noisy doughnut and slammed the accelerator to the floor, leaving rubber on the pavement before the tires caught and the car lurched ahead. He overtook her in seconds, but she veered into the vacant lot. Nick hit the brakes, skidding to a cockeyed stop, dove out of the car and sprinted after her.

His legs were longer, more powerful, but God, she could run. Her feet flew and her hair billowed behind her. She'd kicked off her shoes along the way. He saw them fly from her feet, but didn't stop to get them. The lot was thick with tall grasses and weeds, and Nick's legs were getting soaked to the skin. His shoes were so wet it was hard to keep from slipping. Still, he gained on her.

With one final burst, he jumped on her, taking her to the ground in a tackle that was way more brutal than was decent, landing on top of her. Then he rose a little, rolled her over, clasped her wrists in one hand and held them to the ground over her head. She struggled, and he dropped his body weight down on top of hers, stilling her instantly. "Try that again an' I'll tie you up so tight you'll be lucky if you can breathe. You reading me?"

Her eyes flashed anger at him and her breath came in shuddering gasps. "I'm supposed to come along peacefully, is that it? You want me to load the gun for you, too, before you blow my head off?"

It was the most she'd spoken more than a few words to him, and Nick was surprised that her voice was deep and sultry, not soft and high-pitched as he would have expected from someone her size. She had a voice like Hepburn or Bacall. A voice that—a voice that distracted him from the matter at hand, dammit. "If I wanted you dead, you'd be playing a harp by now." His grip on her wrists tightened when she tried to pull them free. Her breath was warm on his face in contrast to the chill breeze.

She twisted beneath him, trying to wriggle out from under him—a futile attempt. He pressed himself harder against her, his chest jammed so firmly into hers that each shaky breath she drew lifted him. He knew he must be hurting her. He didn't want to hurt her. He didn't want to do a lot of the shit he was required to do at the moment.

When she saw that her struggling was useless, she stopped. He eased the pressure of his body on hers. "What are you going to do with me?" she finally asked.

"Keep you quiet about what you saw in that alley tonight. That's all."

"That's all," she mocked. "You might as well shoot me and get it over with, then. You can't lie on top of me forever." The venom in her voice was real, and he was shocked she could do more than cower in fear and swear she'd never utter a word if he'd only let her go.

"You got a smart mouth on you, lady. I don't need to keep you quiet forever. Just for a few days." His common sense whispered that it might be closer to a few weeks, but he ignored it. What she didn't know wouldn't hurt her—or him.

She seemed to absorb what he'd said and turn it over in her mind. A little more fear came into her eyes. "How do you plan to do that?"

It hit him then that, tough as she came off, she was probably more afraid of him than she'd ever been of anyone in her life. He eased his grip on her wrists and moved off her to let her sit up. He never let go of her hands, though, and he kept her feet in sight at all times. Her question was one he'd been trying to answer since he'd first seen her near the alley. No matter how he figured it, there was only one solution. He stood and pulled her to her feet. "Come on." When he tugged on her, she resisted. Her bare feet braced in the wet grass, she refused to move a step. He turned to look at her.

She squared her shoulders and met his gaze. "No."

His brows shot up as she surprised him yet again. "What do you mean, 'no'?"

"Do what you have to, mister, but don't ask me to make it any easier."

Nick shook his head, unable to understand her train of thought. He pulled the automatic from beneath his coat, intending to persuade her to be a little more cooperative. When he looked at her again she stood straighter and closed her huge dark eyes. Her lashes brushed her cheeks. She looked like a proud Mayan princess about to be sacrificed for the good of her people or something.

Her voice trembling, she said, "Not in the face, okay?"

"*What?*"

"It will be easier on my sister, when she has to identify what's left of me." She opened her eyes again. They shimmered, staring at a spot in the distance. "Just consider it a...last request." When he said nothing in response, she looked him in the eyes. "Could we get this over with? I never thought I'd go out bawling, but if you drag it out much longer, I—"

"Hell!" He thrust the gun back into the shoulder holster and grabbed her again. "Will you get this through your thick skull? I'm not gonna to kill you. You have trouble with English or something?"

Eyes flashing wider, she exploded in a burst of Spanish, none of which he understood. He supposed he could probably guess at most of it, though. He hadn't meant his remark as a racial slur.

Her stream of insults ended. She drew a breath and whispered, "I speak English better than you do, you overgrown thug. I was born ten miles from here. My father practiced at—" She bit her lips as if to stop herself. That aroused his curiosity.

"Go on?" He wondered what her old man practiced and hoped it wasn't law.

She averted her gaze. "What are you going to do with me?"

So she wasn't talking. All right. He could find out anything he wanted to know in less time than she would believe possible. "Got no choice. I'm taking you home with me." He said it slowly, watching her face.

She looked up fast, her shock in her eyes. "You're kidnapping me."

He said nothing, just held her arm and started tugging her back toward the big black car whose headlights and wipers fought a losing battle against the pouring rain.

Toni shivered. She was soaked, she was barefoot and she was mad as hell. How dare this bastard make a remark like that when *he* was constantly sprinkling his speech with "gonna" and "wanna"? Her father may have been Puerto Rican, but he'd also been one of the finest surgeons at Saint Mary's. Her mother had taught English literature at NYU. Toni had grown up hearing both languages, and she spoke both fluently and flawlessly. Her English had no trace of an accent, nor did her Spanish. She was proud of her parents. Mostly. The past had taught her that nothing was more dangerous than an ignorant bigot.

Unless it was being kidnapped in the middle of the night by a hit man. She shook her head slowly as she walked with him back toward the car, knowing there was not much point in fighting him physically. She was going to have to think her way out of this. Months of lurking around courtrooms and reputed mob hangouts had given her a lot to work with. Nothing, though, had prepared her for tonight. Tonight, she'd followed Vincent Pascorelli from the jail. He'd been arrested for conspiracy and had, briefly, agreed to testify against his boss, Lou Taranto in exchange for his freedom. But then he'd suddenly recanted. The D.A. had to let him go, as the charges against him wouldn't hold water anyway. It had all been a bluff. And it had backfired.

She'd expected to see Skinny-Vinnie meet with one of Taranto's thugs, maybe even Fat Lou himself. She *hadn't* expected to get a front-row seat at a hit.

She glanced again at her captor. His long raincoat hung open and his tailored three-piece suit was soaked—ruined, she hoped. At least *he* still had his shoes on. If he hadn't been so damn big, she might have managed to get away from him. She supposed she'd have to make the best of it until she had another opportunity. She was beginning to believe he wasn't going to kill her. It made no sense, but he'd have done it by now if he were going to.

Her foot came down on something sharp, and she winced, lifted her foot, jerked her arm from his grip and ran her fingers over the sore spot. No cut. She supposed she'd live. He watched her, his dark brows drawn together over his narrowed eyes, as she put her foot down again.

The next thing she knew, he scooped her up into his arms and carried her, not over his shoulder this time, but like a hero carries a damsel in distress to safety. Ha! When she tried to fight him, his powerful arms tightened and she gave it up. The guy was just too big. She sat still and clenched her teeth. His jaw was set, she noticed as she watched his face in the rain. Maybe he found this as distasteful as she did. He carried her as if she weighed no more than that gun of his. She wished she was eighty pounds overweight. She wished carrying her would give him a hernia.

This close he wasn't as frightening. Big, yes, but that hardness to his face was only in the expression. He'd lose the hardened-criminal look the minute he smiled, she thought. She could see the shadow of a beard darkening his jaw. He stopped, bending to pick up her shoe when they came to it, and then its partner. As they moved past the glow of the car's headlights, she saw his thick lips and the cleft in the center of the upper one, which gave it a sensual shape, when he wasn't snarling.

He wasn't half as scary as he probably thought he was. He could've killed her. He hadn't. He could've roughed her up, slapped her around until she was ready to do whatever he said. He hadn't. Hell, he couldn't even make her walk barefoot over a lot of broken glass and litter.

When he dropped her onto the passenger seat, slammed her door and started around to his side of the car, she thought about yanking the door open and running again. He must've seen it in her face, because he tapped her window with the gun barrel and shook his head. In another second, he was behind the wheel.

He drove fast, but not recklessly, away from the city. The headlights barely cut a path through the pouring rain. She watched him often. He didn't look her way at all.

He'd driven in silence for forty-five minutes before she drummed up the nerve to ask, "Where do you live? Tibet?"

His brows went up, and he glanced at her briefly

before returning his attention to the highway. "It isn't much farther."

He took the next exit, and they spent ten minutes negotiating side roads before finally pulling up to a tall iron gate. Best she could figure, they were upstate somewhere. He thumbed a button on his keyring. The gate swung open and they drove through. It closed smoothly behind them. The house that loomed ahead was a fieldstone monstrosity. It towered, three stories tall and the color of mud.

He thumbed another button when they pulled up to the attached garage, and an overhead door rose. His headlights pierced the black interior. He pulled the car in, shut it off, killed the headlights. The door closed behind them. They sat in total darkness.

He sighed. She said, "Now what?"

"Don't go nuts on me," he said, his voice very low, as if he thought someone might be listening. "This is for your own good."

She stiffened in anticipation, but he had her wrists quickly imprisoned in one huge hand. His other hand smoothed something sticky over her mouth. Tape! She heard his door open. He pulled her across the seat to get out the same side he had. He kept hold of her wrists and managed to stay far enough ahead of her to avoid her attempts at kicking him. A lot of good it would've done, she thought miserably. She was barefoot

He hauled her forward, flung open a door and pulled her through it.

She was in a kitchen, she realized slowly. It was

dim but not pitch dark. The impression she had was of copper and chrome. He pulled her through another door and along a hallway. She glimpsed a huge formal dining room to the left, and what might be a library to the right. He moved too quickly, his long legs eating up the distance as she jogged in his wake. Another doorway, and she would have gasped if she could, at the living room. A marble-topped bar with crystal glasses suspended upside-down from a rack above it. Brass-legged coffee tables and end tables with glass surfaces. White marble sculptures stood on every one of them: a rearing stallion, a Bengal tiger, Pan with his pipes. The ceilings were stucco, and there was a chandelier with crystal droplets turning slowly. *Money,* the place seemed to say, not in a whisper, but with a boastful shout.

He pulled her along, over plush carpet that felt like heaven to her frozen, bruised feet. She saw a foyer beyond a mammoth archway and what she took to be the front entrance. It glowed with muted golden light, and she caught an unnatural glimmer from the left eye of the bear's head that was mounted on one wall. It caught her attention immediately, and when she looked at it, she realized that the two eyes didn't quite match. Because one of them concealed a camera lens. She'd been at this game too long not to spot surveillance devices as obvious as that one. The question was, who did the big lug want to watch? Or was someone watching him? Did he even know the thing was there?

Her pondering was cut short when they came to

a broad staircase and he pulled her up it behind him. At the top they veered down a hall and mounted still another staircase, this one steep and narrow. At the top of that, they traversed a nearly pitch dark corridor, and went through a doorway into what might have been a study. There was a desk silhouetted in the darkness. Other shapes loomed, but she didn't have time to identify them. He walked her right up to a bookcase at the far end of the room and he reached up and did something to one of its volumes.

Suddenly the entire bookcase swung inward like a door. She felt her eyes widen in fear. Gangsters and hit men she could deal with. Not secret passages in creepy old houses, though. No way. She braced her feet and resisted, but he pulled her hard and she stumbled through into total blackness. The bookcase door closed.

What the hell was this? Was she in some cobwebbed and rat-infested partition between the walls? Was he going to entomb her here and leave her to die where no one could hear her screams? God, this was like something Poe might have written.

He dropped her hands and moved away from her, and she shot forward, simultaneously ripping the tape from her mouth, regardless of the sting. She grabbed for his arm, and when she touched it with her groping hand, she clung. "Don't leave me in here. You can't—"

She stopped when she heard a soft click and the room was flooded with light. Releasing his arm, she looked around. This was a compact living room.

A brown small camelback sofa and a couple of armchairs were arranged on plush carpet a shade lighter. A giant TV was mounted to one wall. Off to her right, there was a tiny kitchenette. To her left was an open door, beyond which she saw a king-size bed, neatly made.

She heard his deep sigh when he crossed to the sofa, apparently no longer concerned about her getting away. He sat down as if exhausted and leaned his head back. His hair was no longer combed down gangster style. The rain, combined with wrestling her so many times in the past hour, had it curling over his forehead as crazily as her own. It was dark as sable and still damp.

She studied him, her fear nearly drowned out by her boundless curiosity. It had always been her biggest flaw. So her father used to tell her.

She looked at the man again. Her kidnapper. "What kind of a setup *is* this?"

"What's your name?" he asked as if he hadn't heard her question.

She hugged herself as a full-body shudder raced through her, hesitating over the question. If he knew who she was, he'd change his mind about keeping her alive in a hurry. Still, it wouldn't hurt to tell him her real name.

"Antonia Veronica Rosa del Rio." She pronounced it with a perfect accent. As far as recognition went, she knew there would be none. It was a far cry from her pseudonym, Toni Rio.

His stern expression changed. He seemed amused.

The hard lines in his face eased, and his lips curved upward at the corners. "I guess I don't need to ask if you're making it up." He tipped his head back and regarded the ceiling. "Antonia Veronica Rosa del Rio," he mused. "What do your friends call you?"

"Irrelevant, since you're no friend of mine."

His head came down and he fixed her to the spot with deep brown eyes. In this light she could see the lighter stripes surrounding his pupils. "Glad you realize it, Antonia." He watched her for a minute longer. "You're shivering," he said at length, then nodded toward the bedroom door. "Bathroom's through there. I'd suggest a hot bath and some sleep. You can use one of my robes for now."

"*¡Que cara!*"

His brows went up. *"Problemo?"* he asked.

"I'd sooner stay wet." She was shaking harder now, and it wasn't entirely from the cold. He was big. Not big like some guys were big; this guy was body builder big. When he started talking about baths and sleeping and her wearing his robe...well, maybe she was a little more afraid of him than she'd thought. After all, they were alone here. They were isolated, cut off from the world.

He stood slowly and came closer until he towered over her, making her feel as small as a child. Her pride wouldn't let her back away. Her gaze stayed on the knot of his loosened tie. Her lungs slowly filled with his scent and that of the rain on his body.

"Look at me, Antonia."

She did. She didn't like looking into those eyes

so she tried focusing on his lips. The sensual curl of them made them more disturbing.

"If you don't get out of those wet clothes," he told her, "you are probably going to catch pneumonia. I'm not in any position to take you to a hospital right now, so I can't allow that to happen. Now, are you going to take them off, or am I?"

She tried to swallow and couldn't. She wanted to move away from him, but her feet seemed to have rooted themselves through the floor. He took her inaction for defiance. She knew it when he shrugged as if it made no difference to him and reached up to release the top button of her blouse.

Toni drew a steadying breath and told herself to move.

He freed the second button. At the third, his fingertips brushed over the mound of her breast, deliberately, she was certain. The way he slowed his movements, made them a caress, was a dead giveaway.

The contact shocked her out of her momentary paralysis. She balled up one hand, drew back and punched him in the jaw. His head snapped sideways from the impact and she spun around and ran into the bedroom, slamming the door and leaning back against it. She was sure he'd come after her, and God only knew what he'd do then.

CHAPTER 2

Nick stared at the door, rubbing his jaw. She'd surprised him more than she'd hurt him. A grudging smile tugged at the corners of his lips, and he shook his head slowly. Damned if he'd come across many men who'd slug a guy his size—let alone one who happened to be packing a 9 mm. Little Antonia didn't hesitate. She was gutsy; no denying it.

At least he'd managed to figure out what she reacted to. He'd been worried about how the hell he was going to control her. His gun hadn't seemed to intimidate her, or his size, or his best street-thug imitation. When he touched her, though, that was a whole other story. When he'd trailed the backs of his fingers over the soft swell of her breast, her pupils had dilated until her irises vanished. Then she'd decked him. Hard.

So he'd learned two valuable methods of dealing with his temporary captive. He could intimidate her with sexual innuendo, and he'd better duck whenever he found it necessary. He didn't imagine there were many things that scared her. He figured he was lucky he'd stumbled upon even one.

Nick tore his gaze from the door and glanced around the room. She'd be safe here, and no threat to his cover. This part of the mansion had been a safe room, designed by a billionaire with more money than common sense. It wasn't on the blueprints, and when the feds had confiscated it for back taxes, they'd decided it was the perfect place for a low level gangster who allegedly came from big money, to live. He unplugged the old fashioned landline phone, wound the cord around it and tucked it under the couch. It had a secure line and was less easily hacked than his secure cell. He'd take it downstairs later, while she slept. He double-checked the bookcase door—cliché, yes, but also the only way out of this hidden apartment. It could only be opened by pressing the right combination of numbered buttons on the panel beside it. A light would flash and an alarm would sound if anyone tampered with the lock, so there was no chance of her getting away.

He felt a momentary pang of guilt, but forced it aside. It wasn't difficult. What he was doing was far too important to put it at risk just for one woman. So she'd be scared for a while. So her family would go nuts worrying about her. So what? Kids were dying every day, and Lou Taranto was as responsible for that as if he were choking the life out of them with his own fat hands. Nick's own brother... No. He wouldn't think about Danny—not now.

Too late, a voice whispered from within, and the memories crashed over his mind like a flash flood.

Nick squeezed his brother's skinny, limp hand tighter, as though he could squeeze the life back into it. "Don't die on me, man. You're all I got, Danny, hold on. Hold on for your kid brother."

Blue eyes opened, but they were filmy—glazed. Danny didn't look like he used to. He was thin as a rail, his face and body, heroin-ravaged. "S-sorry, Nicky...let you down...you kep' tellin' me... poison, man... poison."

Sirens screamed nearer, louder, until they tore Nick's brain apart with their noise. The wind blew like frozen death into the condemned, rat-infested heap Danny and his addict pals called their own. None of them were there now, though. Danny's "friends" had run off and left him there to die alone. Nick reached down to brush an auburn tangle from Danny's forehead. Even if the color of his hair had faded. Danny had all the Irish blood in him, from their mother. Fiona had walked out two years ago—just left. They didn't need her, though. They had each other. Nick was the image of their father, but he didn't want to be. A. J. Manelli was doing eight to fifteen in Attica. They didn't need him, either.

"Help's here, Danny. You hear me?"

There were voices and thundering feet now. Flashing lights bathed his brother's haggard face in color. Red and blue. The cops were there, too, then. Nick felt tears on his cheeks and swiped them away. "They're here, Dan-o. It's gonna be okay. You'll be fine—home in time for your eighteenth. We'll party like we planned. It's gonna be okay."

Only it wasn't.

Nick shook himself free of the rage he'd felt in the months following his brother's death. He'd blamed Danny's friends, but he'd only been sixteen then. Street smart but naive. Those kids, he learned later, had been just like Danny. Young, cocky, following the pack. It was the filth responsible for putting the heroin onto the streets who ought to pay. And Nick knew who that was.

"And pay he will," Nick muttered. "If it causes an inconvenience to one brown-eyed spitfire, that's just too damn bad."

He realized that water was running into the tub. Maybe she was going to take that hot bath he'd suggested. He hadn't expected her to comply quite so easily. Maybe he'd scared her more than he thought. He told himself that was a good thing. She'd be more cooperative, and a hell of a lot less trouble, if she were afraid of him. God help him if she ever got it in her head that he was all bark and no bite. She was cocky enough as it was. She wouldn't be, though, if she had a clue how much trouble she was in. Nobody—*nobody*—eyeballed Viper doing a hit and lived to tell. That Lou Taranto had trusted Nick enough to send him along on one of Viper's jobs was the best thing that had happened since Nick had come in. And that had only happened because Lou knew someone was informing on him, and was suddenly distrustful of everyone in the gang.

To think all his work had nearly gone to hell because one beautiful girl just happened to be in the wrong place at the wrong time!

Nick's stomach growled, and he glanced at his watch. Midnight, and he hadn't had a bite since lunch. He wondered briefly whether Antonia had eaten dinner tonight, then shook the thought away. It didn't matter to him if she was hungry or not.

The water gurgling and splashing into the bathtub covered any noise she might have made scrounging for items she could use to defend herself, if it came to that. She'd found nothing. Not a can of hair spray—he obviously wasn't the hair-spray type—or even a razor blade. The jerk used an electric one. It lay beside the basin, still dusted in tiny black hairs.

She stared at the shaver and frowned. Why in the world would he shave in this bathroom? Third floor, hidden-away apartment tucked behind a wall in a mansion fit for a king. Why use *this* bathroom? She pondered if for a long moment, then had to hurry to shut off the faucets. The tub was nearly brimming.

Steam curled from the water's surface, and she had to admit it was tempting. There wasn't a muscle in her entire body that didn't ache from running, struggling with him, and riding in his trunk. She was chilled to the bone and her feet hurt. The bathroom door had an old fashioned lock and a keyhole. He probably had a key. She'd been in there quite some time already, though, and he hadn't bothered her yet. Maybe he wouldn't.

The robe that hung from a hook on the door was

black velour. It probably came to his knees, but on her it would hover around mid-calf. Maybe ankle. Still, it looked plush, warm and inviting. Biting her lip, she turned the lock. She took a big towel from the pile stacked nearby and placed it within easy reach. At least she'd have something to cover up with if he decided to come barging in. She peeled off her wet blouse, shimmied out of her skirt then exhaled as she lowered her aching body into the soothing bath.

Heat seeped into her, easing her knotted muscles and chasing the chill away. She leaned her head back, closed her eyes and realized that she had needed this. It was the perfect prescription to help her calm herself, assess her situation and begin to make a plan.

"I'm being held prisoner by a hit man," she mused, very softly in case the overgrown thug was listening. "So obviously my first priority is staying alive. Ranks right up there with finding a way to escape."

She slid lower in the tub, until her head was submerged, soaking her hair. When she resurfaced she reached for a nearby bottle of shampoo. It wasn't a new bottle, as you'd likely find in a seldom-used guest room. It was half-empty. She allowed that information to take up residence in her brain for possible future use.

"The question is, do I really *want* to escape? When am I going to get this close to the Taranto gang again? This is a research opportunity like nothing I've ever had."

Her last tell-all book, sold under the guise of fiction, had blown the whistle on several key members of a Colombian drug cartel. Government officials who, for one reason or another, had been dragging their feet on the investigation had been forced to act. Her sources for the book had all been genuine, her information checked to the last detail, and she'd handed every bit of it over to the DEA... just prior to book's release date, giving them time to round up the bad guys and haul their asses in before they realized they'd been outed by a writer.

The pen truly was mightier than the sword.

She'd changed the names of the players in the book, of course, but she'd made sure the people who mattered got the real names, places, dates, recordings, and so on. Of course, the story revolved around ex-KGB operative turned American agent, Katrina Chekov. *All* her books revolved around Katrina. The last two had hit bestseller lists nationwide.

"And this one will be the topper," she mused aloud. "Katrina infiltrates the Taranto crime family." She almost laughed. If Mr. Macho out there had any idea it was Toni Rio soaking in his tub, he'd probably have a stroke. Rumors about the subject matter of her next book were rampant, and the mob was getting nervous. Luckily Toni had always protected her identity. She accepted telephone interviews only, and everything else was handled through her agents and lawyers. If her face became familiar, she'd never be able to move in the right circles and get the information she needed to make her books authentic. In a way, she *was* Katrina.

She shook her head. No, she wasn't. She'd *like*

to be Katrina. Katrina had the courage to do things Toni could never do. While Toni snooped and eavesdropped behind the scenes, Katrina stormed the front gates and faced whatever was behind them. While Toni dreamed of finding the perfect man and having a home and a family, Katrina dressed in slinky gowns and seduced dangerous rogues. Katrina had all the courage Toni lacked. If Katrina had been Tito's daughter, she would never have watched in stunned silence as her father was slowly destroyed. She'd have done something about it.

He hadn't been a great guy. He hadn't even been a very *good* guy. But he'd been her dad, which was more than any of the other daughters he'd sired ever got from him.

Toni blinked her guilt away and rinsed the soap from her hair and face. It had trickled into her eyes and it burned. She ignored the impulse to rehash her dad's decline and fall, or to mentally list all the things she should have done but had failed to do. It was too late for any of it to make a difference now.

She needed to concentrate on the matter at hand. Being who she was and what she was, she probably ought to stay right *where* she was, and consider this a golden opportunity. Swallowing hard, she thought again about the man in the next room. She was afraid of him, might as well admit it. Hiding was something at which she'd become adept, but she felt it as much as anyone else. Maybe more. She wished, not for the first time, that she had a fraction of Katrina's spunk.

She rinsed her hair again, just for good measure—it was so long and thick it required extra care—then leaned back against the cool porcelain to think. It didn't look as if she *could* get out of here at the moment. She probably ought to escape at the first opportunity, though. She couldn't write the book if she got herself shot in the head and dumped off a bridge somewhere. Even if the giant in the other room had decided to let her live, that could change in a heartbeat if he ever found out who she was. So, while there might be a good measure of cowardice in her decision, there was at least an equal measure of practicality.

In the meantime, she decided, there was no reason not to keep her eyes and ears alert. As long as she was stuck here, she might as well get something out of it. And she couldn't do that by cowering in a corner and shaking like a wet dog.

When the water began to cool, she stepped out of the tub, rubbed herself dry and pulled on the oversize robe. The sleeves were too long, and she had to keep pushing them up while she rinsed her underwear in the sink basin. She was arranging her panties on the towel rack to dry when he knocked on the door.

She only glanced toward it and scowled, but he thumped again.

"Antonia? Did you drown yourself in there?"

She lip-synced his words back at him and hopped up onto the counter to wait. It would be a good idea to know for sure if he had a key to this room. She heard him swear and move away after he pounded once more. Seconds later he returned and maneuvered a key into the lock. He pushed the door open, saw her sitting there and frowned as if puzzled.

Toni tried not to show her disappointment. She tossed her wet hair over her shoulder, slid down to the floor and shouldered past him into the bedroom. He was behind her a second later. His hand touched her elbow, and she resisted the urge to pull it away. There was no sense in letting him see how intimidated she was by his touch—how it reminded her of his size and strength. He propelled her into the kitchenette, where a pedestal table held two plates of food. He waved to one of them, and warning prickles raced one another up her spine.

Steak oozed juices and columns of delicious steam. Plump baked potatoes rested beside the meat, and small dishes overflowing with leafy green salad completed his offering. He moved to the refrigerator and stood in front of it, holding the door open. "I have italian, ranch or catalina."

Right. And he expected her to buy into this? "I'm not hungry."

He closed the fridge, a bottle in his hand, and turned to frown at her. "At least try the salad."

Toni's gaze slid from his eyes to the salad bowls on the table. "You must think I'm an idiot." She prayed her false bravado wouldn't fail her now. "Let me correct that notion for you. I won't be eating anything you try to feed me. You'll have to think of something more original." There was a numbing certainty in her mind that he'd put more than salad into the bowl reserved for her.

He stared for a moment before he understood. "You think I drugged it, don't you?"

Her cold, level voice deserted her. She couldn't come up with a fitting reply. A sickening mass writhed in the pit of her stomach when she thought of how easily she could have simply sat down and dug in. This was like walking blind through a pit of cobras. She'd have to watch her every step.

"I don't quite know how to get this through your head, Antonia, but I brought you here to keep you alive."

That really *was* too much. Her temper came into play, and her paralyzing fear was forgotten. "You brought me here to keep me *quiet*, so don't try putting any noble motivations on it. I think we might as well dispense with this bull about a couple of days, too. We both know you have to silence me permanently. A few days won't make a helluva difference, unless you've figured a way to resurrect Vinnie Pascorelli from the dead."

His eyes widened. He lunged forward, one long stride bringing him to her, and he gripped her upper arms and glared into her eyes. "How the hell do you know his name?" He asked the question softly, but his face looked dangerous.

Toni felt her heart flip over. She'd blown it with her damn temper again, and it wasn't the first time. Now what? "I...must've heard you say it to the other guy while I was playing dead."

She watched him turn that one over, trying to remember if anyone had mentioned the victim's name. She waited. He must not have been sure, because he let the matter drop. He continued holding her arms, though. "I need to know if you have a family. Anyone who's going to miss you."

She thought of Joey, the only one of her half-sisters she had contact with, had built a relationship with, and her anger flared anew. "You think I'd tell you if I did? Would you have to silence them, too?"

He released a short breath and shook his head. "You mentioned your sister. How long before she realizes you're missing?"

She eyed him and she felt her defiance oozing from every pore in her. The day she'd breathe a word about Josephine to this bastard would never come.

"I don't want to silence her, Antonia. I only need to—" He broke off there, released her arms and looked at the floor. "Hell, I don't suppose I'd tell, either, if I were you." He reached for one of the salad bowls and pushed it toward her. "I'm not going to poison you, Antonia. Eat your salad."

With an angry swipe of her hand, she knocked the bowl to the floor. Cherry tomatoes, lettuce, slivers of onion and cucumber chunks littered the place like confetti. His face turned murderous. He grabbed for her again, but she was faster. She ran into the bedroom and slammed the door as she had before. He came after her this time. He threw the door open so roughly that she was knocked away from it. He stalked toward her, rage marking his every movement. Grabbing her by one arm, he jerked her toward him until her chest was pressed to his. He held that arm so tight his fingers burrowed into her flesh and she winced. His other hand went to the back of her head, and he twisted a handful of her hair around his fist. He yanked once, pulling her head back. She felt tears of pain and fear burning her eyes.

Then his mouth descended. He was brutal, making sure he hurt her, forcing his tongue into her mouth. She twisted away, but another tug at her hair forced her compliance. His tongue invaded her mouth, attacking, plundering. Her lips were ground between his teeth and her own.

When he finally lifted his head away, she knew there were tears pouring down her face. She tried to check them and found she couldn't.

"Have I made my point?" He let his hand fall from her hair but still held her upper arm, forcing her to face him.

She met his triumphant gaze with tear-blurred eyes. "You made your point. You're bigger than I am, therefore, you're in charge. What you say is law and I'm at your mercy. Is that the point you wanted to make?" She rushed on before he could say another word, angrier than she had ever been in her life—with one exception. "Now, I'll make mine. If you close your eyes in my presence, I'll slit your throat. If you lose track of your gun, I'll use it to blow your head off. If you forget to lock the bathroom door while you're bathing, you might find a toaster landing in the water beside you—plugged in. And if there *is* any poison floating around this hole, you can bet *you'll* be the one who ends up ingesting it. Have *I* made *my* point?"

She doubted her words had much impact, since she blurted them with angry tears streaking her face. He released her arm, shook his head in exasperation and turned toward the door. "Get some sleep," he muttered. "I'll spend the night on the couch." He turned and left her standing there, feeling as if she really could carry out those ridiculous threats she'd hurled at him. She felt as if she could happily wring his neck with her bare hands, if she could get them around it.

And the truth was yes. Her half-sister Joey *would* know she was missing. She would know almost instantly. She might even have known it before it happened.

Nick went to the table and attempted to eat, but the little witch had ruined his appetite. She was being about as uncooperative as was humanly possible and she was only hurting herself. His little show of aggression had scared her into submission—for a moment. His lips thinned and his stomach twisted when he recalled the sight of twin rivers of tears burning down her face. He'd scared her, all right. He'd terrified her, acted like a crazed maniac, made her fear and despise him. He had no doubt she'd meant what she'd said. She might very well try to slit his throat in his sleep, if he gave her the chance. And he wouldn't freaking blame her.

He sawed off a piece of steak and speared it with his fork. "Good, let her hate me. That's just the way I want it." He lifted the fork to his lips, paused, then threw it down in disgust. Surging to his feet, he took two steps toward the bedroom door, then stopped himself. What am I going to do, go back in there and apologize? he asked himself. Tell her I'm not the bastard she thinks I am? *You have me all wrong, lady. I'm a nice slime bag.* Right.

He *could* just tell her the truth.

Nick shook his head the minute that notion popped in. No way. He was already beginning to wonder if her appearance earlier had been an accident. That alley wasn't in what he'd call a good neighborhood. So what was she doing there? How had she known Vinnie's name? She sure as hell hadn't heard it from him, and he knew she hadn't been close enough to see the man's face. He couldn't have mentioned the name. It was too well-known, had been plastered all over the papers since Vinnie had been busted on a trumped-up charge. The D.A. had put a scare into Vinnie, leaned on him until he'd agreed to testify against Lou Taranto. Then at the last minute, Vinnie the songbird had changed his tune. There wasn't a person in the city who couldn't guess why. Lou had got to Vinnie while he was inside. Lou scared Vinnie a little more than the D.A. did. Vinnie recanted. The D.A.'s bluff was called. He'd never had a stand-up case against Vinnie to begin with, so he'd turned him loose. Then Lou sent his top hitter to repay Vinnie for his loyalty. By the time Nick got to the alley to witness the hit, Vinnie was already dead.

Nick remembered the fear in Antonia's face when she'd seen Viper level his gun at her. That had been his first glimpse of her, standing in the rain, trembling with fear and revulsion. No wonder she didn't want to eat. If he could guarantee the food was safe, she probably wouldn't be able to eat it.

Two hours later the light flashed near the door. Nick flicked on the big-screen monitor, reminding himself to hide the remote control when he was finished. The screen lit, giving him a view of the front gate and the pizza truck parked beyond it. Carl stood beside the truck, pressing the button there.

Antonia was asleep. Nick had peered in a few moments ago. He depressed the button on the speaker and spoke softly. "Yeah?"

"Pizza delivery, Mr. Manelli."

"Extra anchovies, kid?"

"Sausage and mushrooms, just like you ordered."

He'd given the right answer. Carl was alone. Nick used another button to open the gate and watched the monitor as the truck lumbered through and stopped near the front door. Nick used the remote to switch the view on the screen to that of the foyer as Carl came inside.

When Nick let him into the apartment a few moments later, Carl tossed the pizza box on a table and glared at him. "I knew you wanted him bad, Nick, but not this bad. How could you do it? How could you pop an innocent like that? She was just..." He swallowed hard and looked toward the ceiling. "She was such a little thing." He closed his eyes, cleared his throat. "The suits are gonna have a ball with this one, Nick."

"Then you were there."

"Vacant room over the bar. I saw the whole thing go down." His gaze was accusing. "I never thought you had it in you—"

Nick pressed a finger to his lips and Carl instantly went silent. He glanced around as if he expected to see Fat Lou emerge from the shadows with an Uzi. Nick walked to the bedroom door, opened it slightly and looked through. Antonia lay on his bed with the covers pulled protectively up to her chin. Her hair spilled over his pillow, completely hiding it from view. Her thick black lashes touched her cheeks. He stood back and allowed Carl to peer through the crack in the door. Carl did, then he pulled back in shock, and Nick closed the door again, urging his friend away from it.

"What did you *do?*"

Nick sat down on the couch, stretching his legs out fully and tipping his head back. "The only thing I *could* do. You didn't really think I'd shoot an innocent bystander, did you?"

"What was I supposed to think when I saw it with

my own eyes?"

Nick shrugged. "She *was* convincing, wasn't she?"

"What, you just told her to fake it and she did?"

Nick didn't want to relive the tense moment. "I told her I'd kill her if she didn't."

"And she just came here with you? How much did you have to tell her?"

Nick's head came up. "I didn't tell her anything, Carl. She already knows too much. She saw Viper."

Joey paled visibly. "I was afraid of that. It's as good as her death warrant, you know that, Nick."

"Exactly. I brought her here because I had no choice. If *I* didn't have one, how the hell could I give her one?"

"You kidnapped her."

Nick winced at the term. "I'm trying real hard to think of it as protective custody."

Carl shook his head, got up and went to the refrigerator. He took out two beers, tossed one to Nick and popped the top on his own. "Man, I'm relieved. I thought you finally went over the edge." He took a long drink from the can. "So do you think Lou trusts you, or was it a test?"

"No way to tell, although if anyone identifies Viper to the local cops in the near future, you can bet my body won't be found for months."

"You know how many people that bastard's killed, Nick?"

Nick nodded slowly. "I know. I want him put away as badly as you do. Now that I've been at the actual scene of a hit, I can give sworn testimony and take Viper out of commission for good. Maybe." He hadn't seen the actual hit, though, dammit. "But we have to let him have his head a while longer if we want to take Taranto out, too." Nick sat a little straighter. "How's your part in the drama coming along?"

"I'm still just one of Taranto's low-level gophers, running errands for the big boys. I did wrangle an invitation to a poker game tomorrow night at the Century. Word is there's something big coming up. I hope I can find out what."

Nick frowned at the news. The Century was Lou Taranto's nightclub—a place where most of the patrons were mob players and prostitutes. Private rooms were commonly set aside for invitation-only poker games. Every employee in the club was drop-dead loyal to the Taranto family. "I don't like it, Carl. You'd have no backup. What if something goes wrong?"

"What do you think I am, a rookie? I've been at this as long as you have. You know damn well the bureau's got guys watching Lou's place twenty-four hours a day, snapping cameras and taking down names. An extra plain-brown wrapper parked out front won't raise any eyebrows. Lou's so used to having them around, he sends out sandwiches sometimes. They don't worry him any. I had Harry assign somebody in case I get into trouble. All they know is that if they see someone stand in the left front window and flick a lighter three times before lighting his smoke, they raid the place and bust everyone inside, me included, for gambling."

"But the surveillance guys won't know there's a Fed inside," Nick said.

"They don't need to know. That's the deal."

Nick shook his head. "I still don't like it." He saw the determination in his friend's face and sighed. "At least you'll have a way out."

"Right. Now, what are we gonna do about the girl?"

It was just like Carl to change the subject rather than risk an argument. "I'm keeping her here," Nick told him.

"Not a smart move, my friend."

"Smarter than letting her go. The second she was spotted, Viper would kill her."

Carl sighed. "You're right on that count. If he knew she was alive, a whole army couldn't protect her from that bastard. But, God, Nick, how long can you keep her here?"

"As long as I have to." Nick frowned at a small noise from the bedroom. He met Carl's glance, his eyes conveying a warning. Was she up and listening? They'd kept their voices low, and Nick wasn't concerned about his cover. Still, it wouldn't hurt to buy some insurance. His voice only slightly louder, he added, "I just hope she's not foolish enough to try and escape. She'd be digging her own grave."

Toni didn't close her eyes after that. She couldn't

believe she'd managed to fall asleep in the first place, knowing he was just in the next room. All she had to do was think of him to feel his mouth possessing hers again. He'd enjoyed showing off his physical power over her. The truth was, she was glad he'd done it. There had been odd moments when she'd actually found herself thinking he was attractive, admiring his size and the hardness of his body. Of course, she hadn't allowed such thoughts to linger. For all she knew, he was a killer. Well, good. She wouldn't think of the man as anything but repulsive from here on in. He couldn't have done anything to turn her off more.

She pushed all of her analysis aside and tried to guess who had been speaking to him just now. She'd been roused from sleep by a man's deep laughter and she'd quickly pressed her ear to the door. She'd heard "Carl's" question, "What are we going to do about the girl?"

And the answer: "I'm keeping her here."

Nick. Carl had called her captor Nick. Then she heard both men remark on her abbreviated life expectancy should she be discovered by Viper. Was Nick telling the truth, then, when he said he'd brought her here to keep her alive? More likely to keep himself alive, she thought. He would be a marked man if Viper ever learned of his little deception. Neither of them mentioned killing her. She supposed she could take that as a good sign. And the bit at the end about digging her own grave had obviously been tacked on for her benefit. She wasn't an idiot.

A few minutes later there had been absolute silence. Either Nick had left her alone or he was asleep. She was too afraid to open the door to find out which was the case, so she went back to the bed, where she still lay, wide awake, in the morning.

She knew she was a wreck when Nick flung the door open. Her eyes were sore and felt puffy. Her head ached from lack of sleep and nervous tension. All things considered, she'd had better mornings.

He stepped into the bedroom with a flash of straight white teeth in that tanned face and a tray of food in his hands. Toni sat up, clutched the robe tighter and watched him warily. His eyes scanned her face, and his smile vanished.

"You didn't sleep?"

"Did you really think I would?" She injected all the venom she could into the words.

Instead of getting angry, he only frowned harder and put the tray down on the bedside stand. When he sat on the edge of the bed, she intended to slide right out the other side, but he gripped her wrist, his hand capturing hers with the speed of a cobra striking. "You look awful."

"Sorry. Being kidnapped has that effect on me."

"More like no sleep and nothing to eat."

"Who's to blame for that?"

"Look, I'm trying to be friendly," he snapped. "Why don't you lighten up? I brought you breakfast in bed. How bad can I be?"

"I've already told you, I won't eat anything you bring me." She said it louder than she needed to, but the aromas coming from the tray were too cruel to bear.

"Use your head, Antonia. I could think of a hundred more practical methods of killing you than poison."

"That makes you an expert, doesn't it?" She averted her face to avoid the tempting scents. "Take it away."

"Maybe you think it's something other than poison. Is that it?" He caught her face in his hands and turned her until she faced him. "You think I dropped a roofie in there? Think I want to knock you out and have my way with you?"

She felt her cheeks blazing and tried to pull free of him, but he held her still and smiled. "You are a bastard," she said slowly, enunciating each syllable.

"You may be right." He let go of her face. "But at least I've figured out a way you can eat." He pulled the tray of food nearer the edge of the stand. She couldn't resist looking. The brown sausage links and fluffy yellow eggs pummeled her senses. Her stomach rumbled and he laughed. "What would you say to a brief truce? Just long enough to eat breakfast?"

She glanced at him, her eyes narrow with distrust. He took a sausage and brought it to his lips, his eyes fastened to hers. He took a bite from the end. She couldn't look away as he chewed, swallowed, licked his lips. He held the same piece of sausage to her lips. "Eat, Antonia. You're hungry and you know it."

Ignoring her pride, she parted her lips and let him push the sausage between them. She took a bite. He smiled and she realized she was staring at him instead of the food. He was so different this morning, speaking softly. His face was relaxed, not hard and scowling. His hair wasn't wet or slicked back as it had been, but dry and thick and wavy, with a shine to it that rivaled a mink. He wore a faded pair of jeans and an ordinary T-shirt—clothes that accentuated the muscles underneath.

He took another bite of the sausage and held the last tiny piece in his fingers. He pushed it into her mouth, and when she took it, her lips closed around his fingertips. A jolt shot through her at the sensuality of the contact, and she didn't miss the dark intensity in his eyes.

He looked away quickly, scooped eggs onto a slice of toast, folded it and took a bite. He handed it to her this time. He didn't try to feed her from his hands again.

Toni was famished, and more grateful to him than she cared to admit for thinking of a way to show her the food was safe. She shouldn't be. It was his fault she had to be suspicious of everything he said or did. She ate everything on the plate, always careful that he tasted first. She even made him sip her coffee after she'd added cream and sugar to it. He grimaced but he sipped. He drank his own black and bitter.

"This is much better," he said, relaxing now and sipping his coffee. "I think we got off on the wrong foot last night, Antonia. This will work out better if you think of yourself as my guest. I promise I won't keep you here a day longer than necessary."

She was shocked at his easy, almost friendly tone. "It isn't that simple. There's my si—" She stopped herself.

"Your sister," he finished. He drew a breath and released it slowly. "I wish I could do something about it, but I can't."

"She'll be worried." Antonia saw the compassion in his face and pressed him. "Couldn't I send her a note—tell her I've gone away—"

He shook his head. "She'll have you back alive. It's the best I can do. Sorry."

"Not the best you *can* do, only the best you *will* do, you lousy—"

"Nick," he told her. "It's Nick Manelli. Save yourself the effort of thinking up all those lovely nicknames, okay?"

He drained his cup, stood and left the room. When he returned he carried a large green plastic trash bag. "I brought you some things to make your stay a little more bearable." He dropped the bag in the center of the floor. "If I've forgotten anything, let me know and I'll do my best to get it for you." He stepped back into the living room and closed the door.

Curious, Toni got up and looked inside the bag. She drew back in shock. Her own clothes lay in neatly folded stacks. Her purse rested on top. Gaping and gulping air as her rage mounted, she flung open the door and charged him.

"You arrogant bastard! You broke into my apartment last night! You—"

He held up one hand, flat palmed. "I did not break in. I had a key. It was in your purse along with the address. If you recall, you left it in the trunk last night when you kicked me and ran like hell. The least I could do was get some of your things for you. It was no trouble. You don't need to thank me."

"Thank you! Thank you? I—"

"You're welcome, Antonia. I knew you'd appreciate it. Of course, I am beginning to think I shouldn't have bothered bringing a robe. You couldn't possibly look better in it than you do in mine." His gaze moved heatedly down her body.

In her fury, Toni hadn't tightened the cord. The robe hung loose to her waist, and the inner swell of her breasts had caught his gaze. She tugged the cord tight and moved toward him. "You are the lowest, most vile, son of a—" She'd lifted her hand in preparation as she spoke, but he grabbed it in mid-swing.

One ruthless tug, and she was flat against him. "Since I've already demonstrated what happens when you lose that hot little temper of yours, I can only conclude you want more of it."

Her eyes focused on his lips, and her anger began to turn to fear. "Thanks for reminding me what a scumbag you are, Manelli. For a second there I thought you might have a crumb of decency."

"Never think that, Antonia, because I don't. Push

me too far, and you'll find that out." His eyes blazed down into hers, and Toni waited, trying not to let the moisture spring into her eyes.

CHAPTER 3

Her tears were his undoing. She didn't let any spill over; she was too proud to do that a second time. He saw them all the same. They formed glistening pools that made her black eyes into rare and exotic gems. Something rose up inside him, pushing the breath from his lungs, and Nick dropped his arms and turned away, shoving one hand through his hair.

"I'm doing my level best to make this easy on you, lady, but if you want it rough, make no mistake, I can make it rough." His voice was unnaturally gritty. He didn't care. He only knew he had to get away from her. He blocked her view of the panel with his body as he punched the numbers in, then went through the door without looking back once.

On the other side, after slamming the bookcase closed behind him, he stood still for a second. What the hell had just happened in there?

He went back over the confrontation in his mind, trying to pinpoint the moment when the tide had turned against him.

He'd been ready to kiss her cruelly, just to show her that she shouldn't be trying to slap a guy his size every time she got her dander up. He'd almost done it. Hell, it had worked the first time.

But when he'd had her there, crushed against him, and he'd looked down to see her storm-tossed eyes, something had slammed into him. He'd felt her heart pounding, and he'd been suddenly, acutely aware of his own, pounding right back. He'd heard her short, choppy breaths, and lost his own. Her scent had enveloped him, *she* had enveloped him until he was aware of nothing else—only her. If he hadn't stepped away, he knew damn well what would have happened and he was not happy about it. He would have kissed her—but not the way he'd kissed her last night.

In his soul, he knew he'd have slipped his arms around her until he could cradle her head in his hands. He could imagine the feel of all those silken, raven curls tangling around his fingers. He'd have tasted her lips first, drawing them between his own. He wouldn't have bruised them this time. He'd have worshipped them. He'd have—

Nick groaned and forced her golden skin and wild black mane from his mind. She must be some kind of witch, he thought. An elusive enchantress capable of casting powerful spells over men. At least, over him. What was he supposed to do with her for the rest of the time he had to keep her here?

He shouldn't be having this problem. He'd worked in close proximity to some gorgeous women in the past. He'd *never* had a problem. He'd always been perfectly able to take them or leave them. Never had he felt so close to losing it—as though he'd been shoved off a cliff and was scrambling for a branch to keep from falling.

"Chemistry," he muttered. "Major chemistry."

Turning from the bookcase door he went down to the second floor and the master bedroom. Since she'd cycloned into his life, he figured he would have to use this bedroom often. Before, he'd only done so frequently enough to make it appear lived-in. He'd have to force himself to keep her out of his thoughts for the rest of the morning. Lou Taranto and Viper would be here to see him soon, and he'd damn well better be on his toes.

If sending him to witness the hit had been a test of Viper's loyalty, then Viper had passed with flying colors. If it had been a test of Nick's loyalty, on the other hand.... he figured he would soon find out his grade. If he'd been sent because Lou trusted him, he'd learn that, too. Those were the probable reasons for this sudden visit from the boss.

Nick grimaced as the third possibility entered his mind. If Viper or Lou had any idea that Antonia was still breathing, Nick would be a dead man in the next few minutes.

Carl knows she's in the apartment upstairs, he thought grimly. If anything happens to me, he'll come for her.

Still, his own particular preference was that he get to keep on living.

He peeled his shirt over his head and tossed it carelessly as he moved into the adjoining bathroom for a shower. Despite his decision to keep Antonia out of his thoughts, he recalled his late-night visit to her apartment as he stood beneath the pounding spray. He hadn't learned a lot. He'd had to get in and get out as quickly as possible and do it without being seen. His reasons for taking her things had been twofold. He wanted her to have everything she needed and he couldn't afford to be seen buying women's clothing and toiletries in a store. That was the first reason. The second was her sister. While it was necessary that the woman, whoever she was, act worried about Antonia's disappearance, Nick had to give the sister something to cling to. With enough of Antonia's belongings missing, maybe she could believe Antonia had just taken off for a few days. The sickening worry could be put off for a little longer. It wasn't much, but it was the best he could do.

The apartment was nice, but not exactly spic and span. There had been a day-old newspaper spread on the counter that separated living room and kitchen. A stained coffee cup sat there, as well as a cereal bowl with the spoon still inside. A couple of blouses were slung over the back of the brocade sofa. Antonia wouldn't win any housekeeping awards.

Nick had moved quickly to the bedroom to get the clothes she'd need. He found the bed made, but haphazardly. The comforter was neat, but the sheets underneath showed bumps and bulges. He took an empty suitcase from her closet but didn't bother packing it. It was faster to drop the clothes into the trash bag he'd brought along. Taking the suitcase was just to make her impromptu vacation a little more believable. He took the book she'd been reading from her nightstand, too.

He moved into the bathroom, where she'd left a towel slung crookedly over the shower curtain rod. He took her toothbrush and everything else she might conceivably need. Before he left, he'd checked the one remaining room, probably another bedroom, behind a closed door but when he tried the door, he found it locked. He frowned. Why keep a spare bedroom locked?

He would have pursued the matter, but the sound of the telephone—a landline—split the silence like an ax splitting a melon. It rang again, and Antonia's voice filled the apartment, so low and sexy it was as if she was in the room.

"...can't come to the phone right now. Leave a message and I'll get back to you."

Nick listened. Maybe he'd learn something about Antonia after all. A woman's voice came clearly.

"Hey, Toni. I loved reading about Katrina's latest. Can't wait to see what that vixen will be up to next." There was a long pause, then, "Look, sis, I've got a bad feeling. And you know that's a big deal, for me, so if you don't call me back, I'm gonna have to come looking." The woman sighed. "I wish you'd move upstate, closer to me. Call me, okay? I love you." The line went silent, and Nick continued to stare at the machine.

Sis.

Her sister. It had to have been her sister.

I love you.

Nick sighed as he noticed the framed photo near the phone. Antonia–Toni–arm in arm with a blonde who looked nothing like her. Or maybe...yeah, a little bit around the eyes. They both wore "I'm the evil sister" T-shirts and were smiling. Their eyes held real love for each other.

A rush of scalding pain filled his chest. He'd been that close to his own kid brother. He hated worrying Toni's sister like this. But dammit, it couldn't be avoided.

It returned to him all over again, that pain, as he stood in the shower of his phony home preparing for a meeting with his phony boss, the man he held responsible for his brother's death. He had to focus on Lou Taranto and Viper, on playing the part he'd spent months creating.

He'd never had the chance to see what was behind that locked door in Toni's apartment. People had been coming and going in the hallways and he'd decided to get out before he was discovered and questions were asked. He couldn't stop thinking about the message on the machine. And he was curious as hell about that other name Toni's sister had mentioned. Katrina. Who was she?

But he couldn't spend any more time dwelling on

any of that. Lou was on his way, would be there any minute. He twisted the knobs, stopping the water flow, and stepped out. After toweling down, he dressed in one of the expensive suits he kept in the closet, and combed his hair back while it was still wet. Personally, he thought it made him look as though he was stuck in a time warp, but he did it anyway. It was part of the image, he supposed. Helped him to look like the gangsters had looked in all the movies he and Danny had watched as kids. Kept his head in the game, kept him from breaking character. And that was important. Breaking character, in this case, would get him killed.

Toni paced the small living room and wondered if he was deliberately trying to confuse her. He'd been about to deliver another rapacious kiss, crushing her lips and devastating her mind. She'd seen it in his face—but then it had changed. He'd softened visibly. His hold on her had eased until it was more like an embrace. The anger in his eyes had vanished, and the emotion that had taken its place, for the tiniest space in time, had looked like raw desire.

How would she have responded, she wondered, if his kiss had been tender, driven by attraction rather than anger?

Insane! Even the idea was insane. She wouldn't let herself think about it again. It was obvious that he was playing some kind of mind game with her—

trying to convince her that, though he worked for the most powerful criminal in the state, maybe the country, he was really just a nice guy. Why else would he have taken the couch and let her have the bed, or shared her food so she wouldn't go hungry? It was all part of his ploy to confuse her—and it was working, she realized.

She forced the overdeveloped jerk out of her thoughts. Let him be as nice or as mean as he wanted. It wouldn't matter to her one way or the other. She occupied her mind fully with unpacking her clothes and finding places to stow them in the bedroom. She squashed his things to one side of the dresser drawers, trying but failing to picture him in the brilliant-colored basketball jerseys she found there. She shoved his things to the back corner of the closet and hung some of her blouses and sweaters in front of them. She glimpsed a pair of basketball shoes with neon laces in them and shook her head. They clashed with her image of him. She shouldn't be surprised, though. Anyone built the way he was obviously worked out to get that way.

She hadn't thought about it before. There must be a whole other side to Nick Manelli, associate to the mob. Toni's insatiable curiosity was thoroughly aroused. Why the hell was she wasting time unpacking clothes when she should be giving this place a complete once over. Who knew what kinds of things the guy was hiding?

Dragging a chair nearer the bedroom closet, she stood on it to see what was on the top shelf. At first she noticed only a couple of spare blankets and a well-worn basketball. Then she poked around some more, moving things aside to search behind them, and her fingers met something hard. A photograph in a frame, she realized as she pulled it down.

She sat on the chair and studied the faded black-and-white snapshot. A man, a woman and two little boys smiled back at her. The woman seemed young and happy, and the boy on her lap bore a striking resemblance to her. But it was the man who caught her attention. He was the image of Nick Manelli, in every way except one. He didn't have muscle bulging from every possible locale. He was lean, lanky. She let her gaze move down to the little boy standing in front of the man, and she knew she was looking at Nick. He couldn't have been more than six years old, with a wide grin and a tooth missing. His hair was a riot of dark curls beneath his father's hand. A lump formed in her throat. How did an adorable child like that, from a beautiful family like that, grow up to be a common criminal?

She was getting distracted again. She stood and put the photo back where she'd found it, then completed her examination of the bedroom, noting little of interest except the far smaller TV. Of course she'd seen it there before, but she hadn't given it any thought. Now she did, though. Why have two televisions in an apartment this small?

In the living room, the first thing she looked over carefully were the rows of books. It hadn't occurred to her to wonder if any of hers were among them, but it did now. Her heart was in her throat as she scanned the spines on the two shelves along the wall. Not that he could recognize her just because he'd read her book. It just made her uncomfortable to think he might have one here. As it turned out, he didn't. She sighed her relief and frowned. There was one small area where the books were not pushed back to the wall. A space had been left behind them. She had to stand on a chair again, and in seconds she pulled a slender remote control from behind the books.

Why would anyone hide their remote?

She got down, knowing she was onto something. She had that tingling certainty she got from time to time. Maybe a shared gene with her half-sister Joey. Like a bloodhound, Toni always knew when she was on the right trail.

She pointed the remote at the big TV and pressed the power button. The image that lit the screen was even more confusing: a tall iron gate, standing motionless on a twisting drive. She stared, blinked slowly, and then the truth hit her. This TV was serving as a closed-circuit monitor—probably hooked up to the camera she'd noticed in the bear's head, as well as several others. She tested her theory by hitting the channel button. Just as she'd suspected, each click gave her a view of another part the mansion.

"He must have a camera hidden in every room," she whispered, still flicking through channels. She stopped when she saw the living room with the black leather furniture and marble-topped bar. Nick stood at the bar, pouring whiskey into heavy crystal glasses. He was, once again, the gangster she'd seen in the alley. He wore a dark suit, minus the jacket. His hair was slicked down. His stance, his very expression, were different than when he'd been in the apartment with her.

Beyond him she saw Viper, his beady eyes darting constantly in his puckered little face. He stood near a fat man with white hair and flabby jowls. Toni knew him. She would have known him anywhere. Lou Taranto. She thumbed up the volume button, and it worked. She could listen to them, as well.

Nick forced a smile for his guests, but it felt stiff. All he seemed able to think about was that Antonia was only two floors above them. Having Viper this close to her chilled him right to the marrow. He splashed Johnny Walker into three ice-filled glasses, despite the early hour, and handed them each one.

Lou took his and held it up. "To new associates."

Nick clinked his glass to Lou's, and tried not to show his relief. He was pretty sure he was the "new associate" Lou was referring to, and that meant his cover was still intact.

Viper didn't raise his glass. He apparently wasn't thrilled with new associates in the least. He was cautious. More so than Lou. Nick looked at him and felt the same bristle of aversion he'd felt from their first encounter. Trying to avoid becoming this man's enemy was essential if he was going to get the evidence he needed to put Lou away and take down his organization. It was also the toughest thing he'd ever done. The guy was a snake.

"You get Vinnie dumped okay?" Nick asked, trying to sound friendly, but not weak.

"Yeah, sure. No problems." Viper took a slug of the whiskey and smacked his lips.

Lou shifted from one foot to the other, watching them both, his eyes missing nothing. The guy was sharp.

"Somethin' wrong, Lou?" Nick asked. "You look uneasy."

"The girl. Where'd you dump her?"

"She's in the bay." Nick tried not to show his reaction to the question. Did they know something? "Weighed her down real good. She won't turn up for months. Maybe never."

Lou nodded, looking fractionally easier. "Who was she?"

Nick shrugged as if it didn't matter.

"Dammit, Nicky, didn't she have any ID on her? Didn't you check?"

Nick took a long pull from his glass. The less Lou knew about Antonia, the better. "Didn't think it was important. She saw us, she had to go. There was no time to check her out before I hit her, and after I just wanted to get her the hell outta my trunk before I got stopped or something." He shrugged. "Doesn't matter anyway. Dead's dead, Lou."

Lou grunted and didn't say anything. Nick felt a

cold finger of unease trace the curve of his spine. Finally Lou sipped his whiskey and sat down, his substantial weight noisily crushing the leather cushions. "Viper tells me Vinnie went down easy. You agree?"

"Viper didn't wait for me. It was a done deal by the time I got there."

"But you're sure it was Vinnie? You took a look at his face before it was...altered?"

"Sure did, Lou. No mistake. Vinnie the songbird in the flesh."

"He won't be singing anymore," Viper put in. He laughed aloud, and Lou did, as well. Nick forced himself to join in.

"What about the body?" Lou drained his glass, got up with an effort and refilled it from the thousand-dollar bottle without asking. He was speaking to Nick.

"Lou, I couldn't watch the dumping. I had to get the girl the hell outta there. Some nosy shit had already called the cops."

"You don't need to send witnesses on my jobs, Lou," Viper snapped. "You know I always come through. Vinnie's feedin' fishes."

Lou nodded, still standing. "Let's hope he's a lesson to the next rat who thinks of squeaking to the D.A." Nick raised his glass and nodded hard. He downed the rest of the whiskey in a slug that burned a path down the center of his chest.

Lou cleared his throat. "Things'll be hot in the city for a while—as soon as they miss Vinnie."

"They knew what they were doing when they sprung him, Lou. They didn't care. He wouldn't give the testimony he promised, so they just didn't care. And they call us the criminals." It was the longest speech Viper had ever made in Nick's presence. The worst part was, he was right.

"Sure, but no one's gonna admit that," Lou said. "It'd be political suicide. Besides, it gives 'em a great excuse to hassle me. When did you know 'em to pass one up?" Lou shook his head, frowning. "At least it's what I expected. I don't like surprises. That's why I'm worried about that girl. She was a surprise."

"Too bad Nick was in such a hurry to off the bitch," Viper said slowly. "I could'a made her tell me her life story." He licked his lips. "She was a looker, Lou. We could'a kep' her awhile—like we did with that uppity hooker who tried to put the squeeze on you. 'Member her? But Nick, he's got a hair trigger, this guy."

Nick's jaw clenched tight, and he felt a muscle work near the corner of his mouth. He turned slowly and glared at the slime standing across from him.

Viper met the scorching gaze with one of his own. Lou was quick to step between them. "I don't think Nicky likes you findin' fault with his work." His tone made the simple statement a reprimand. He glanced at Nick. "It's okay, Nicky. I think you done good. Hell, Viper said she was off and running when you popped her. If she'd have got away, all hell would'a broke loose."

"Funny, though," Viper said, slow and confident,

his snake's eyes never leaving Nick's face. "I drove by there this morning and I didn't see no blood."

"You saying she didn't bleed, Viper? Or are you saying something else?" Nick took a step closer to the little weasel, his temper approaching the boiling point

"I'm saying I'd feel better if I'd'a had a look at her before you took off. How do I know she's dead? She saw my face." Viper stepped closer as well, and Lou's pudgy body was wedged between them.

"Maybe you'd like a trip to the bottom of the bay yourself, pal. Maybe you'd feel better if you saw her up close and personal." Nick leaned over Lou, his voice level but tight.

"Enough, already." Lou's command cut the tension between them and Nick backed off. "I got enough trouble without you two going at it like a couple of punk kids." He nailed Viper to the spot with his gaze. "Nicky says he killed her. That's good enough for me. I don't want to hear you talk him down again."

"You're crazy, Lou. He's not even one of us—"

"But he will be." That statement earned stares of disbelief from Viper and Nick. Lou turned and encircled Nick's shoulders with one beefy arm. "Next commission meeting is this weekend, Nicky. When it's over, you'll be a made man—officially."

Viper downed his whiskey and slammed his glass on the bar. "You really think that's a good idea, Lou? Nick isn't proven."

"He took the broad out." Lou slapped Nick's

shoulder repeatedly. "For me, he did this. He acted from loyalty, and loyalty to Lou Taranto doesn't go unrewarded. You should know that." His arm tightened, and he grinned until his fat face puckered. "What do you say, Nicky?"

"I'm honored, Lou. I—I wasn't expecting this."

Lou reached into a pocket and extracted an envelope that appeared stuffed to the bursting point. He pressed it into Nick's hand. "A little thank you, for the girl, Nicky. You done good."

Nick accepted the money, thanked Lou, but his thanks were waved away. "I need a favor," Lou told him. "Like I said, things'll be hot in the city. The Century won't be practical, and we need this meeting. This place—" he waved an expressive arm to indicate the entire room "—this place would be perfect."

Nick swallowed and tried to appear bowled over with joy that the leaders of several organized crime families would be meeting here. The idea shook him. These guys were sharp. But he had no choice. You didn't thumb your nose at an offer like this. It was an honor. To refuse would be taken as a personal insult, and Viper was already suspicious of him.

"My place is yours, Lou."

"Good, then. Saturday night. And don't worry about the vote. I'll speak to the others. They'll fall in line." He gave Nick one last slap on the back, put his glass down on the bar and turned toward the door without another word.

Viper glared at Nick. "Don't get too cocky, Manelli. The vote isn't over yet, and if I have anything to say about it, you'll come out on the short end."

"Lucky for me you don't have anything to say about it, then, isn't it, Viper?"

Toni's stomach convulsed when she heard Viper talking about how he could've "made her talk." Thank God Nick had been there.

She brought that thought to a grinding halt. Nick was no hero. He was only the lesser of two evils. He'd taken part in a murder. No, she corrected herself. He'd arrived in the alley after the fact, if she could believe what she'd just heard. Still, he was about to be inducted into the mob.

She watched him after the crime boss and his favorite henchman had gone. Nick turned in a slow circle, pushing one hand through his hair and rumpling its slick perfection. He looked stunned and more than a little bit worried. He ought to be, she thought. If those two found out what he'd done— that he'd lied to them and hadn't killed her at all— he'd be a dead man.

He really *had* taken a risk in not letting Viper shoot her that night—or letting him take her alive and do far worse. There was no way she could deny it. Nick had saved her life. According to the slimy Viper, he'd saved her from more than just death—a lot more.

But why?

He moved as if deep in thought, picking up glasses, replacing the whiskey bottle, wiping the bar with a soft cloth. Toni was sure of just one thing. She wouldn't leave here now—not even if he left the doors wide open and offered her a ride to the bus station. The bosses of at least three major crime families would be meeting under this very roof. She had this wonderful setup to watch them and listen in. To turn her back on a research opportunity like this would be nothing short of pure cowardice. She couldn't let fear chase her away from this. She'd leave here somehow, soon, but *after* that meeting. She ought to be able to survive four more days here. Nick obviously wasn't planning to kill her. He wouldn't have risked his life to keep her alive, only to kill her later. She'd be fine as long as he never guessed who she really was.

She glanced at the screen, stiffening when she saw only an empty room. Shit, he must be on his way back. Quickly, she shut the TV off, jumped up onto the chair and replaced the remote in its unoriginal hiding place. The she placed the chair exactly as it had been before and ran into the bedroom to finish unpacking so she'd appear busy when he returned.

She pulled the last armful of things from the bag and stuffed them into an already crowded drawer. That done, she bent to pick up the bag, surprised to find there was still weight in the bottom. She bent and pulled out the last items in the bag: two brand-new spiral notebooks and her own copy of *On Being a Writer*. She'd left the book on her nightstand beside her bed.

Did he know? My God, had he been inside her

office? The office door was always locked, but there were copies of every book she'd ever written in there—and in the safe behind the framed painting of her first cover, there was enough evidence to put Lou Taranto behind bars for the rest of his life. If Nick had found it, he would kill her. There was no chance he'd do otherwise. She should have turned it over to federal authorities, she moaned inwardly. She'd known that was the right thing to do, and she'd come perilously close to handing it to a cop she'd later learned was on Taranto's payroll. She'd been terrified to make the same mistake again.

Did Nick know now that she was Toni Rio? He must. Bringing the book and the notebooks were his way of telling her the game was over. She held the books in hands clenched tight and white knuckled.

"I found it in your bedroom." She jumped as if jolted and spun to face him.

CHAPTER 4

Toni stood motionless, unable to utter a word, waiting.

"Look, the truth is, you might be here for more than a few days," he went on. "I figured if you could get something out of this enforced vacation—spend some time writing, if that's what you want to do with your life—it might be easier on you."

She opened her mouth and closed it again, still unsure.

He shrugged. "You've got to start sometime, Antonia, or you'll never know whether you're any good."

She thought he must have felt the air currents stirring when she sighed in relief. He'd bought the notebooks so she could try her hand at writing.

Pretty nice thing for a morally bankrupt criminal to do.

He's probably still trying to confuse me, she reminded herself.

"I could've sworn you just smiled," he said slowly. "Did I finally do something right?" As he spoke, he turned toward the dresser, snagged his tie loose and tossed it. He looked tired—drained. His gaze met hers in the mirror, and his lips curved slightly in response to her alleged smile. She caught just a trace of the whiskey's aroma clinging to him.

"I suppose, if I had to be abducted and held against my will by a two-bit hood, I could've done worse than you."

"Don't heap such extravagant compliments on me, lady. You'll swell my head."

She smirked at him, her relief that he hadn't discovered her secret making her feel easy for once in his presence.

"Before I forget again," he continued, facing her. "Who is Katrina?"

She felt the blood drain from her face. "K-Katrina... who?"

"Damned if I know. You had a message on your machine last night—a woman. She said something about wanting to know what Katrina was up to."

There were only two possibilities that came to mind. Her agent or her sister. She swallowed hard, wishing she could hear the rest of the message. "Katrina is, um, an old friend. I've known her since I was a little girl." That much was true. Before Katrina had developed into an ex-KGB super-sleuth, she'd been the imaginary friend of a four-year-old. Later she'd been a fictional big sister Toni used to threaten bullies. Way back before she'd learned that her father's wandering libido had provided her with several real sisters. She'd learned about Joey only two years ago, looked her up and they'd formed a real connection. According to Joey, her mother had alluded to the likelihood that there were others, but they had no clue how to find them.

As a child, Toni used to blame Katrina for her own offenses. "She's a rather adventuresome lady," she said at length. She glanced up to see if Nick believed her. He seemed to be accepting what she said. "Did the caller say who—"

"It was your sister. She called you Toni. It fits you."

The air left her lungs. Toni sank slowly to the edge of the bed, her eyes on the floor. She'd hoped Joey wouldn't miss her right away. She lived upstate, four hours from the city Toni called home. Hell, she wondered how close she might be to Joey right now. They'd definitely driven upstate, and quite a long ways. At least an hour.

"Did she...did she sound worried?"

His gaze slid away from hers. "A little. For what it's worth, I took enough of your stuff to make it look like you'd gone away for a few days. If she checks, she'll think—"

"She'll know." Toni closed her eyes slowly and tried to remind herself that Joey Bradshaw was not exactly a fragile flower who needed protecting from difficult topics. In fact, if Joey knew where her half sister was right now, she'd probably hop on her Harley, drive here, kick the door in, grab Nick

Manelli by the scruff of his neck and give him a swift kick in the *cojones*.

"You're *that* close?" Nick's voice made it sound as if she'd just claimed the impossible.

Toni opened her eyes slowly. "She's my *sister*." She shrugged. "Besides, she...knows things."

He scowled and shook his head. She had the distinct impression that he did not believe her. She could have kicked herself for the overwhelming urge to convince him, and still she found herself doing just that. "Maybe we're closer than most, but that's because we need each other. My parents died young and so did hers—"

"Wait, I thought you were sisters."

"Half." She was telling him too much. She paused and drew a shaky breath. "I've only known about her for a couple of years, but in that time she's become my best friend." She sought Nick's face and found it with an expression of sadness, his gaze still focused on her. He was listening—*raptly*.

He pulled his gaze away and tried to sound casual. "What kinds of things do you do together?"

His voice had come out minutely tighter than before, and Toni wondered why. "Everything we have time to do when we visit each other."

"She doesn't live in the city then?" he asked.

She bit her lip, didn't answer.

"I'm not trying to get information on her, Toni. I saw the photo on the phone stand in your apartment. You look...close."

"We are. She's been great to me, and I don't want

to cause her all this worry."

"She won't worry much. There's no sign anything bad's happened to you."

"Of course she will. For God's sake, wouldn't *your* brother worry if you dropped off the face of the earth without a word?" He sent her a sharp look and she quickly added, "I mean, if you had a brother. Or a sister. Do you?"

His eyes narrowed, but then he looked away. "Not only would he not worry, he wouldn't know. My brother is dead."

"I'm sorry." She thought of that photo, that little boy, and her heart broke. "What about...your parents? Where are they, Nick?"

Nick's voice was devoid of emotion, his expression shuttered, but he answered her question. "Our mother walked out when I was thirteen, and I haven't seen her since."

Toni swallowed hard, the image of the woman in the photograph reappearing in her mind. How could she have walked out on her own sons? "Again, I'm sorry."

"I'm not." He released the top buttons of his shirt and stalked into the living room. Toni followed.

"Then your father raised you alone?" She shouldn't be so curious about his background. She certainly didn't care. But he'd lost his father and brother— she'd lost her parents. The only difference was, he pretended not to care.

He walked to the little speaker doc that sat on the bookcase, tapped the touch screen on the tiny iPod in its cradle. In a moment Ray Charles' voice sang, "Georgia... Georgia...." and Nick sank into a chair. He leaned back, hands behind his head, legs stretched in front of him, and closed his eyes. "Last I knew, my old man was doing eight to fifteen in Attica. He went up when I was still a kid."

"Then he could be out by now, couldn't he?" Toni felt her stomach turn over. Had his father gone to prison before his mother had abandoned him or just after? She couldn't help seeing the sweet, dark-haired little boy in the photo, with his front tooth missing, and feeling the incredible hurt he must've felt then.

Nick shrugged. "I never bothered to find out."

"What was he—"

Nick's head came up. "That's enough, Antonia. I'm not up to telling you my life story, and I can't imagine why you'd want to hear it." Again he tipped his head back and folded his arms behind it.

Toni took a seat on the sofa and studied him. The tension in his body seemed to be ebbing. He'd been wound up and nervous from his encounter with Taranto when he'd first come in. Now the mellow piano and the soothing voice coming from the Bose system seemed to be calming him.

"You like the blues," she said, unconsciously keeping her voice low, out of respect for the music. "I never would have guessed."

"Relaxes me."

She shifted, feeling anything but relaxed. "Was it whoever was here before that got you all tensed up, or talking about your parents?"

He didn't move. "You don't know when to quit, do you? Okay, I'll bite. How'd you know someone was here?"

"It was a guess. I saw the red light come on, by the panel."

His head moved enough to nod. "Sharp lady."

"Are you going to tell me who it was?"

"What do you think?"

Antonia sighed and got to her feet. He'd given away all he was going to. Her stomach protested softly, and she realized it must be nearly noon. "Am I allowed to help myself to some lunch?"

He nodded. "Can you cook?"

"It is not one of my more highly developed skills. I was thinking along the lines of a sandwich or some cottage cheese." She walked to the refrigerator and scanned its contents. "Or some yogurt," she said, spying the row of containers.

"Help yourself."

Toni hesitated, then shrugged. "You want one?"

"Why not?"

She picked peaches and cream for her, strawberry banana for him, located two spoons and carried them back to the sofa. She held the plastic cup out to him, and he took it. Their fingers touched and for a moment that seemed eternal, Toni didn't take her hand away. When she did, she felt flustered and not sure what to say.

Something had passed between them. Some unspoken agreement or understanding. He wouldn't hurt her. She'd be safe as long as she was with him.

He'd been saying so all along, but she was sure of it now. She didn't quite hate him anymore. She was beginning to see that there were reasons he'd become what he had—strong emotions that had shaped him into the man he was. If he was bitter, it was no wonder. He was alone in the world. And she knew what that felt like.

He seemed content to relax there with the music filling the room. Toni was eager to write down some of the interesting discoveries she'd made here and begin to fit them into her plot and Katrina Chekov's world. She hesitated, though. The fact remained that she was Toni Rio and her book would ruin Lou Taranto. If Nick found out, all bets were off.

She finished her yogurt. "You speak any Spanish, Nick?"

"Not a word," he said, taking his last bite. She couldn't seem to take her eyes from him as he licked the pink cream from his lips. "Although I can tell when you're swearing at me." He got up at long last, carried the cup to the kitchen sink and rinsed it. "I have to go out again. I might be a while."

Toni sighed loudly.

"Don't tell me you'll miss me." He was mocking, but not cruelly. It was almost a friendly sort of teasing.

"In your dreams, I might," she replied in the same tone. She took her cup to the sink as he had, rinsed it, then turned, leaning her back on the drain board. "I don't like being locked up here alone. There's not a window in the place, not a soul to talk to—"

"There's music," he said. "There are all those books." He pointed at the shelf. "Besides, you can use the time to do some writing. If you get sick of that, there's a TV in the bedroom—"

"What's wrong with this one?" Toni couldn't resist asking.

"Not working right now," he replied without missing a beat.

Toni chewed the inside of her lip. "If I spend every day sitting in this apartment, I'll gain twenty pounds inside a week. I run every day, for God's sake. I can't vegetate for God knows how long just because it's convenient for you."

He crossed his arms over his chest and leaned against the fridge. "Piling it on a bit, aren't you? It's only been one day."

She smirked at him. "I thought you'd understand. *You* obviously work out—"

His brows shot up. "Not much slips by you, does it?" His amusement stirred her anger, but not for long. "How about a deal?"

Her curiosity rose up on its hind legs. "What kind of deal?"

"I have a basement gym. You behave yourself while I'm gone, and I'll take you down there."

"When?" She sounded too eager, but she couldn't take it back now. She truly was beginning to feel like a caged animal.

"As soon as I can. But right now I have to go." Toni sighed in resignation, while he perused her face.

He stepped closer, looked down at her, smiling

slightly. "I wouldn't be averse to a kiss goodbye, if you're interested."

"Since when do you ask permission?" She tried to make her answer sting, but her eyes went to his full lips the minute he asked the question.

He shrugged. "Is that a yes?"

"Only if you'd like to kiss my knuckles, Manelli."

He nodded, his face splitting in a broad grin. "Atta girl. For a minute there I was afraid you might be losing your spunk." He tousled her hair playfully as he spoke, then his hand stilled, buried in her curls. He took it away slowly so the long tendrils slipped between his fingers. Toni pushed off from the sink, ducked under his arm and moved quickly to the bedroom where she'd left the notebooks.

She picked them up. "I'll take your advice and do some writing, then. See you later." She closed the bedroom door.

A moment later she heard him leave and she relaxed again. She'd have to be careful or she'd wind up liking the man. She'd have to keep reminding herself that no matter what kind of horrible childhood he'd had, it was no excuse for what he did now. Lots of people had lousy family lives and still managed to grow up and become productive citizens.

She was surprised that she was able to put him out of her mind and concentrate on writing. The words flowed from her at a remarkable rate. Time slipped by without her being aware of it. Pages filled, one after another. She wrote in Spanish so he wouldn't be able to read it and guess what she was doing.

Nick couldn't explain why he'd told her the things he had. He talked to no one about his family. He didn't even allow himself to *think* about them. None of it mattered; it was in the past and that's where it should remain. It had no bearing on his life today. With one exception. Danny's death was at the core of his need to end Lou Taranto's reign as king of the underworld. The man had been getting rich on other people's suffering for too long. It would end. Nick would be the one to end it.

He ran the errands necessary that afternoon, taking the money Taranto had given him to three different banks to exchange it for clean bills. It wouldn't surprise him if Lou had somehow marked the bills and was keeping track of them, so he had to treat the money the way he would if he were as dirty as it was. As dirty as he was pretending to be. He then went to a small gym and left the clean money in an envelope in one of the lockers.

He told himself he shouldn't be thinking about Toni all alone and restless in his apartment. He shouldn't allow her to haunt his thoughts the way she was. He shouldn't keep catching phantom traces of her scent on every wayward breeze. He shouldn't unconsciously rub his fingertips together, remembering the feel of her hair. He certainly shouldn't keep imagining how it would feel to hold her against him with nothing between his skin and hers.

Nick blinked fast, shocked at the path of his thoughts. He and Toni had come to a tentative truce, if he'd read her right this morning. He couldn't revert to total animosity between them by coming on like a caveman again. He'd get a lot more cooperation from her if he could keep things friendly between them, but not too friendly.

By the time he returned to the hulking mansion, it was dusk. The sky beyond the house was only a shade lighter than the house itself. The place looked haunted. Big and dark and ugly. It wasn't a home— not anybody's home, but least of all his. It was just a cover. Something the government set him up with to help convince Taranto he was a productive criminal. The truth was, Nick didn't have a home. A small apartment in Brooklyn served as a base when he wasn't undercover. He wasn't sure he wanted a home. It would be too damn empty.

He picked up the white paper bag with the cartons of Chinese food inside and hurried up the two flights to the apartment. When he went in, Antonia was on the couch with her legs curled beneath her. She was bent over a notebook, her pencil flying over a page. She was so engrossed, she didn't even hear him. He quietly set the food down and went back through the door to pick up the landline telephone he'd left in the study. He carried it inside and closed the door, and still she didn't look up.

His curiosity got the best of him, and he walked up behind her and glanced over her shoulder, frowning when he saw line upon line of Spanish. So she didn't want him reading what she wrote? Interesting.

"Productive afternoon?"

She looked up fast and slammed the notebook closed. Her eyes had a spark in them that he hadn't seen before. It was like the effect of certain amphetamines. He had the feeling as she looked at him that she wasn't really seeing him, but was instead still at least partially immersed in whatever she'd been writing. "I didn't mean to interrupt. You look... driven."

"It's going pretty well," she told him. Her gaze fell to the telephone tucked under his arm, and the zealous gleam left her eyes entirely. "I've heard of portable phones, but isn't that a bit much?" Her attempt at humor was lame, at best. It didn't fool him for a second. He set the phone down, cursing himself for bringing it in now when he should have waited until she was distracted in another room. It was cruel to let her see it when he couldn't let her use it

He grabbed up the bag and took it to the kitchen. "I brought food. You like Chinese?"

"It's fine." Her voice sounded dead.

Nick sighed hard. He walked to the couch and sat close beside her. "What is it?"

"Nothing." She looked everywhere but at him.

He cupped her chin and pulled her head around so he could see her eyes. His thumb traced her jawline of its own will. "You might as well say it, Antonia. Your face is too expressive."

She pulled her face from his grasp. "You have the telephone," she said slowly. "It would be so easy to let me call her." She got to her feet, restless.

Her sister again. He'd actually thought he'd won that argument. "I would if I could. I'm not doing this just to be cruel, you know." He stood, as well.

"You could let me call if you wanted to. Just plug the damn thing in—stand beside me with your gun to my head. Blow my brains out if I say one wrong word. I just want to let her know I'm okay—"

He gripped her shoulders, silencing her tirade. "Use your head, will you? If your family doesn't act worried, it will be obvious to Taranto that you're still alive."

"Taranto doesn't know who or where my sister is. He doesn't even know my name," she whispered. "How can he watch her if he doesn't know who I am? Unless...you're going to tell him."

He released her and threw his hands in the air. "Of course I'm not—dammit, I thought we were past this stage. I'm not going to tell him anything about you, but that won't stop him from finding out. And when he does, you can bet he'll watch your sister. If she acts suspicious, he'll do more than just watch her. It would be just like Lou to assume she knew where you were and try to make her tell him, and if that happens—"

He stopped when he saw the change in her. Her eyes narrowed. Her jaw twitched and she stepped closer to him. Her voice shook with anger. Her breathing was fast and shallow. "If anything happens to her, Nick Manelli, I swear you will pay. If I have to wring your neck with my bare hands, you'll pay, and that goes for your precious Lou Taranto and that snake, Viper too!"

He felt the return of that grudging respect for her just before he felt the shock. "How do you know Viper?" She said nothing, and Nick saw her courage waver. He saw the fear behind it. He stared at her, shaking his head and wondering how he'd been so stupid. "It was no accident, you being in that alley that night. What were you doing there, Antonia?"

She met his gaze. She stood inches from him and tipped her head back to pummel him with her tear-glazed eyes. "I can't let anything happen to her," she said. Her voice was hoarse. "It would be my fault. God, I never stopped to think I would be putting her at risk. I'm not used to having anyone in my life that could suffer from my recklessness. I can't let anything happen. Not this time. I can't stand by and do nothing, like before. I won't. I'll do anything—"

"Stop." She was approaching panic; he could see it swirling in her ebony eyes. "Toni, I didn't say—"

The tears spilled over and he choked. She gripped his shirt in her fists. "Don't let them hurt my sister, Nick. For God's sake, don't let that happen."

He didn't intend to slide his arms around her or to hold her tight against him. It wasn't something he thought about doing. It was something he couldn't help doing. He cradled her head against his chest and he rocked her slowly. Her shoulders quaked. She was stiff in his arms, but she didn't pull away. "I didn't mean it to sound like a threat. I just wanted you to understand why I couldn't let you call her. No one's going to hurt your sister." He held her harder, his arms tightening almost against his will. A lump came into his throat, and he closed his eyes. "I swear to God, I won't let anyone hurt her."

She shook her head as much as his grip on her would allow. Her voice was muffled by the fabric of his shirt, and her breath warmed his skin right through it. "You have no control over what Taranto might do. No one does."

She sounded so hopeless. It tore at his emotions— emotions he hadn't known he could still feel. "Don't be too sure about that."

She sniffed, pulled herself away from his chest but not out of his arms. She blinked her eyes drier and frowned up at him. "What do you mean?"

"I mean I may not control Lou, but he can't control me, either." He saw her brows lift, the need in her eyes. *Make me believe,* she seemed to be begging him. *Take this awful fear away.* "There are things I can do," he said softly, "things Lou never has to know about. You can trust me on this, Toni. No one will touch her."

She stared up at him, her huge black eyes like bottomless pools. But a moment later they clouded, as if she'd only just remembered who was speaking to her. "Trust you?" She whispered. She looked at the floor and shook her head slowly. "Good luck."

Reassurances leapt into his throat, but Nick swallowed them forcibly. To convince her she could trust him would be to destroy his cover. He didn't answer, and when she gazed up again he couldn't face her imploring eyes. He let his arms fall away from her and shrugged. "Fine, don't trust me. You'd sleep better if you did, but that's your problem. In the meantime, why don't you tell me what you were doing in that alley, in the middle of the night, in the pouring rain?"

"I was watching a contract killing," she said softly. "Why didn't you let your pal Viper shoot me? It would've solved all your problems. I saw him lift the gun. He never misses, or so I've heard. What was going through your head when you knocked the muzzle down? Any other thug would've just...." Her head came up slowly, her wide eyes narrowed, and her brows pushed at one another. "Why *did* you stop him from killing me?"

Nick didn't like the look in her eyes. He wasn't sure what was on her mind, but it had him squirming like a worm on a hook. He tried to keep the offensive. "How do you know Viper? No one knows his face."

She acted as if she hadn't heard him. She turned slowly, looking at the apartment as if she were seeing it for the first time. "Why do you stay here, in this hidden apartment? Are you hiding from someone?"

Nick's temper began to simmer. He didn't like the way she was trying to take charge of the conversation. His jaw tight, he demanded, "When did you hear the dead man's name?"

She shook her head slowly as her gaze fell on the phone. "Why do you bring the phone in here every time you want to use it? Why not just use it out there, or use your cell like everyone else in the twenty-first century?"

He turned and paced away from her, more uncomfortable than he could remember ever having been. He could barely believe it when she followed, her hand on his shoulder trying to turn him to face her.

"When do you drink the beer I saw in the fridge instead of that expensive whiskey downstairs?"

"How the hell do you know I had whiskey downstairs? Did you—"

"Smelled it on your breath. I'm observant. And I'm not done. When do you pull on your high-tops and shoot a few hoops? In between dumping bodies and snuffing witnesses for Lou Taranto? Why do you talk like a thug and dress like a gangster when you're with him and speak like a normal human when you're with me?"

Nick was stunned by her barrage of questions and the direction they were taking. He tried to force a scowl instead of showing the shock he felt. "You seem to have forgotten your position in the scheme of things, Antonia. I'm in charge. Your life is in my hands. You'd be on a slab in a morgue right now if I hadn't dragged your cute ass out of the trouble you stepped into. *I* ask the questions. *You* answer them. Is that clear?"

She stared up at him a moment longer. She raked her fingers through her hair and shook her head. "No. I'm crazy to think... Look, I've had all I can handle, okay? I'm going to bed."

She took her notebook, turned and walked away. As soon as the bedroom door closed, Nick slammed his fist on the table hard enough to send the cup that sat there two inches from the surface. She was one giant pain in the ass, and if she was thinking along the lines he thought she was, she was going to be trouble. Her presence in that alley had been no accident. He was sure of that now. That theory was out the window. She knew too much.

"Yeah, way too much," he muttered.

She knew just how to look at him to make him forget about protecting his cover—to make his stomach tie itself into a knot while he broke his back to try to tell her what she wanted to hear. Her tears worked better on him than automatic weapons would. He paced the room and wondered if he should give in to the urge to kick the damn door in and make her tell him the truth.

He had to remind himself that her reasons for being in the alley were probably the least of his problems. She was beginning to see holes in his story. Holes no one else had seen. She had looked at him just now as if she could see right inside his brain and read his mind. It was damn nerve-racking. It reminded him of—

He wasn't prepared for the reality that hit him. It reminded him of the way Danny used to look at him whenever he tried dishing up a line of bull.

Nick sucked air through his teeth at the sudden pain, like a yard-long saber, running him through. He saw his brother's knowing expression. Danny always knew when Nick was lying, used to say he could see it in his eyes shining like a beacon. It drove Nick crazy. He'd been the best liar he knew. He'd had to be, or he'd have wound up in foster care somewhere with Danny somewhere else. He'd made up some of the biggest piles of crap ever once the two of them had been on their own, and people bought it; the wild excuses he invented for school officials whenever they wanted to see one of his parents, the line he'd fed the manager at the High Spot when he scammed his way into his first job.

He'd always been big, so it was easy to convince people he was older than he was. But the club owner wanted an experienced bouncer, not a rookie. By the time he was hired, Nick had convinced his new employers that he was the greatest bouncer in the city. Nick had gone home and tried to tell Danny his new job was at a convenience store, and Danny had seen right through it. Nick had been afraid his brother would try to make him quit, and he loved the job. Tossing guys twice his age out on their butts when they got out of hand was the most fun he'd ever had. He used to fantasize that his father would come in some night. He planned to put the bastard through the door without bothering to open it first.

He'd kept working in that dive for two years after he'd lost Danny, and the entire time he'd been in training. He told himself it was because he had to be tough to keep the job. Deep down, though, he knew he was bulking up so he'd be ready to take on Lou

Taranto and his thugs.

It was only later he'd realized the best way to do that was to go into law enforcement.

Nick forced the mismatched memories from his mind. Why had he thought about his past so much lately—about Danny? Was it just having *her* here that brought the memories on? Was it because he felt, even from his first glimpse of her standing terrified at the edge of that alley, an irrational urge to protect her? Just the way he'd wanted to protect Danny.

He'd known his brother was in trouble, and he'd tried every way he knew to talk him back from the edge. Danny ignored Nick's warnings and walked face first into the fire. He'd left Nick alone, just as their worthless father and mother had. Just as little Antonia would do if he gave her half a chance, he thought, even if it was likely to get her killed.

He wouldn't let her do that.

He shook himself and plugged the telephone in to call Carl. He was already late.

"Yeah, Carlito's Pizza, whaddya want?"

"Sausage and mushrooms to go," Nick replied, to let Carl know that he, too, was alone and free to talk.

"Where've you been, Nick? On vacation?"

"Couldn't be helped. You forget I have myself a new roommate?" Nick glanced up at the bedroom door and wondered if the little snoop was listening. "You have enough money for that card game tonight?"

"Not unless I win the first few hands."

"That's what I figured," Nick said. "Go down to

the gym. I left a package in your locker."

"Greenbacks? Thanks, Nick."

"Thank Taranto. It's what he gave me for handling that little problem the other night."

Carl hesitated. "You—uh—think he might've marked the bills, Nick? If he connects us—"

"I did some banking today. The money's clean."

"Perfect. How's your guest, by the way?"

"Just beautiful. What do you say I send her to your place for a while?"

Carl laughed. "Uh-uh, pal. You caught her, you keep her."

"I was afraid you'd say that. Listen, I need you to call Harry for me. I never know when she has her ear pressed to the door."

"Curious, huh?"

"A little too curious. She knows stuff she shouldn't. She's got a sister, and I'm uncomfortable with her security. I want you to have Harry assign a man to try to figure out who she is and where she is, and make sure she's all right. I want to know if one of Taranto's guys gets within ten blocks of her."

"Got it. Anything else?"

"Yeah. A background check on the lady herself. She's holding back."

"I'll call Harry right now. Then I have to head over to the Century. I'll see you after the game if there's anything worth telling you."

Nick hung up, unplugged the telephone and took it with him when he left. The tension coiled tight inside him hadn't eased any, and he needed to work it off. If he didn't, he thought he was likely to wring Antonia's pretty neck for keeping so much from him. A little voice whispered that wringing her neck wasn't at all what he'd like to do to her.

He felt a pang of guilt on the way down. He had promised her a crack at the basement gym...and he would give her one. To have her with him now would defeat the purpose. She was the source of the tension he needed to get rid of.

Toni hadn't heard his telephone conversation because she'd locked herself in the bathroom to pace and try to work through her new theory. It seemed so obvious all at once. Nick didn't just switch personalities arbitrarily. It had to be deliberate. He was like two men in one body, entirely different with Viper and Taranto than he was with her. She'd been confused by him before. How could he point a gun at her head one minute and buy her notebooks the next? She wasn't confused anymore. She thought she knew the answer.

He wasn't working for Lou Taranto at all. He was undercover, just like she was. He was probably some kind of cop. FBI. DEA. Something.

Joy at her newfound theory bubbled in her chest, and she caught herself grinning. Wait a minute, she thought, pulling a mental emergency brake. Just why does this idea make me so damn happy?

Why shouldn't it? It certainly would improve my odds of

surviving this mess.

It would also ease the guilt she'd been feeling for allowing herself to be physically attracted to a man whose moral values were roughly equivalent to those of pond slime.

Am I saying that it's now okay to feel slightly *attracted to him?*

No way, she realized. She could easily be adding two and two and coming up with eighty-nine. She might only be seeing what she wanted to see and not what was truly there. Still, she couldn't help but feel a hint of relief that he'd made that promise about protecting her sister. If he was a cop, the offer made perfect sense.

And what if he's just a great liar?

She had no idea how much time had passed, but she finally realized she was too wound up to sleep and that her stomach was too empty to relax anyway. When she emerged from the bathroom, Nick was nowhere in sight. She located the Chinese food in the fridge and helped herself to a little bit of it. She no longer feared he'd try to poison her. Besides, he'd eaten from both cartons. She took her plate to the coffee table and wondered if he'd left the house or just the apartment. If she was going to find out who Nick Manelli really was, she would have to keep a close eye on him.

Retrieving the remote control and flicking the TV on, she got comfortable on the sofa. She used the buttons to move from room to room, but didn't see him in any of them. Then the basement gym filled the screen. She choked on her peanut chicken and dropped the remote when her fingers went limp.

She'd found him. He lay on a bench, knees bent, feet flat to the floor on either side. He wore a pair of baggy yellow shorts with an elastic waist and nothing else. His chest was bare and magnificent. He pressed a bar with several disks at each end. His face contorted as he pressed. Sweat made a sheen over his nose and forehead. He clenched his teeth, his lips pulling away from them each time he pushed the bar up, away from his body.

Toni stood slowly, her gaze magnetized by the image on the screen. His arms bulged with each rep. His chest muscles expanded, his pectorals rippling with the effort. She dropped to her knees and felt around for the remote, found it and thumbed the volume control without looking. He grunted with every rep. He didn't count, just emitted a guttural "ummf." The sound seemed forced from him.

She'd known he was big. She'd felt the hardness of his body whenever she'd had physical contact with him. She'd felt the bulge of those muscles under his clothes when he'd held her close to him—but, dear God in heaven, she hadn't imagined he looked like *that*. She could only imagine how he'd feel....

Toni flicked the power button off and sat there, blinking at the now-dark screen. Her stomach had a tiny lead ball resting right in its center. God, her throat was dry. She couldn't swallow.

She went to the kitchenette and opened a cupboard for a glass. She needed to drink something. When she glanced up, the rounded, amber-colored bottle caught her gaze. It lay on its side, bottom facing out, on the top shelf. A plain old bottle of Jack Daniel's, not that expensive stuff he'd been feeding to Lou Taranto. Toni pulled a kitchen chair closer and told herself it was only to help her sleep.

CHAPTER 5

Nick stretched his hour-long workout into two and then some. He hadn't realized just how much he needed it until he got started. By the time he began to feel a little of the tension slip away, he'd pretty much exhausted himself. He spent another hour in the pool trying to cool down and relax.

When he finally showered and went back upstairs, the apartment was silent. He opened the bedroom door and peeked in. Antonia was curled on his bed, breathing deeply. There was a glass with a bit of amber liquid in the bottom on the stand beside the bed. Frowning, Nick moved quietly across the room, picked the glass up and sniffed. Whiskey. She'd been snooping again.

He looked down at her and wondered why she felt in need of a shot. Was she that wrought up over her sister? She stirred and sighed. The light from the living room spilled through the slightly open bedroom door and landed on her hair, so it gleamed like a raven's wing. For one wild second, he had the insane urge to bend over her and kiss her lips—to taste the flavor of the whiskey on them and the flavor of her behind them. He shook himself and turned to leave the room. God knew what she'd think if she woke and found him standing over her.

It was tough to leave, though. He wasn't sure why it gave him such a rush to look at her as she slept. It couldn't have been that glorious hair all over the place, or that she hugged his pillow to her like a lover. It couldn't be because in this light, her skin was the color of cinnamon or that he could see the dampness and smell the soap from her recent shower.

He made himself take a step toward the door. She moaned softly in her sleep, and he stopped.

"Mmm," she murmured again. And then, in a whisper, "Nick."

She could have hit him with a hammer and done less damage. She'd whispered his name in her sleep—and she'd said it as if...

He stepped closer and sat down gently on the edge of the bed. He smoothed the hair away from her face and looked at her. Her eyes opened slowly, and for an elastic moment she gazed up at him, a lazy smile curving her lips. Her hand came up to cover his, where it rested on her cheek. She blinked.

Her eyes flew wide. She yanked the covers to her chin and moved as far from him as possible. "What do you want?"

Nick shrugged innocently. "You called me,

Antonia. I thought something was wrong." He watched her face, making no move to get off the bed. "Was it a dream?"

Her eyes were huge and darker than midnight as she searched her memory. "No!" She shook her head fast, so her hair flew. "I mean, not a dream. A—a nightmare."

He frowned. "That's funny. You were smiling when I came in. Looked as if you were about to start purring." He tried to sound genuinely concerned. "What was this... *nightmare* about?"

She shook her head once more. "I don't know. I really don't remember." She said it quickly, not even bothering to try.

"That's the thing about dreams. They're so vivid and then they're gone." He touched her chin with the tip of his forefinger. "The real thing, Antonia, you'd never forget."

He got up, chuckling, and strolled out of the room. He could feel the daggers she was shooting at his back before he closed the door. As soon as he finished grinning, he asked himself why it gave him such an absurdly huge sense of satisfaction to know that he wasn't the only one having impure thoughts. It certainly wouldn't make things any easier. He couldn't just hop into bed with her and go on about his business.

Why the hell not?

The question stopped him cold. Why not? He'd done it before. What was so different about her?

Dumb question. Everything about Toni was

different. So damn small, she seemed fragile as crystal, and so damn intrepid she was always on the brink of disaster. She was a giant in a tiny body. She was a sorceress, dancing through his mind but always just out of reach. Her eyes were black quicksand. A man could get lost in those eyes and never find his way out.

He paced for a while, then reclined on the couch knowing he'd never close his eyes. How could he, when he knew she was just in the next room, as wide-awake and restless as he was? He shook his head, trying not to think about a sure cure for both of them.

It was a relief when Carl showed up later. Nick reached for the remote, checked to be sure his friend was alone and let him in. The smaller man was flushed right down to the bald spot in the middle of his head, came in pacing, and talking too fast and too loud. Nick had to keep reminding him to keep his voice down.

"Okay, Nick, okay. But this is hot. It's going down tomorrow night and I'm in. I can't let it go. Not this time."

Nick took his friend's arm and urged him into the kitchen, as far from the bedroom as possible. "Slow down, Carl. *What* is happening tomorrow night?"

"Heroin. A big shipment of it, coming in from I don't fucking know where, but it'll be arriving at Taranto's warehouse sometime after nine p.m. Four guys have to be there to unload and I'm one of 'em."

Nick schooled his face into an emotionless mask.

It had been heroin that had killed Danny. Heroin important and distributed by Lou Taranto. "So?"

"Come on, Nick, you know what I'm saying. That stuff will hit the streets in a matter of days, if not hours. Lou has a crew waiting to split it up for distribution, and we both know they'll be selling it in no time. I can't let that go." He shook his head and ran one hand over it, front to back. "We have to look the other way all the time when we're under. I can't do it this time."

"It's your tip, Carl. Call it. We'll play it your way."

Carl looked at Nick for a long moment, his blue eyes thoughtful. "If we let the stuff get inside the warehouse, we might as well forget it. The place is like Fort Knox. A lot of cops would go down in a raid."

"So what do you want to do?" Nick thought he already knew the answer, and he knew he wasn't going to like it. Allowing Fat Lou's poison to hit the streets was unacceptable...but so was losing his best friend. His only friend.

"I'm dropping an anonymous tip to the local cops," Carl said. "Gonna let 'em know when the truck is due in and what it's hauling. They'll be there waiting."

Nick expelled his breath in a rush. "They'll be there, all right, and they'll be loaded for bear. There's no way you can tip them that there's a Federal agent with the suspects. You'll probably end up getting your head blown off."

"Forewarned and all that, pal. I knew the risks

when I signed on. Besides, better I buy it than some kid who ought to know better. Some kid like Danny." He paused to let that sink in. "I figure this way I give the cops a pretty fair chance, with only four guys and the driver shooting back at them."

"Five guys and the driver," Nick said softly. "I'm gonna be there with you."

Toni leaned closer to the door. She had to strain to make out what they were saying because they spoke so softly. They must be in the kitchen. She recognized Carl's voice, but so far, hadn't understood half of what they'd said. She opened the door a crack, better to hear them and hoped they wouldn't notice as she knelt low and peeked through.

"Oh, that's brilliant, Nick. You come along, that way we can both get shot full of holes."

Nick's eyes looked like Toni had never seen them. Possessed or something. "How long's it been, Carl? Huh?" He was almost whispering. "What, twelve years now? You remember when you lost Gina and crawled into a bottle headfirst? It took some doing, but I snapped you out of it."

Carl sniffed. "Smashed every damn bottle I had and wouldn't let me out of your sight for a week."

"Even further back than that," Nick went on, and his voice was gritty. "The night Danny OD'ed. I lost it. I wanted blood and I was ready to get it with my bare hands. If you'd let me go out that night, I'd never have come back alive. You remember? You had to sit on me to keep me from going after Taranto alone. You ended up with a black eye by morning—"

"The way I remember it, you weren't too pretty the next day, either."

"Hell, I had twenty pounds on you even then, Salducci."

"Yeah, but I had ten years on you, you muscle-bound punk."

Toni opened the door a fraction of an inch further. Nick put one hand on Carl's arm. "You stuck by me, Carl. You're the only one who did. It's gonna hit the fan tomorrow night, and I'm damn well gonna be there to tell you when to duck."

"More like *I'm* gonna be there to carry *your* oversize ass home when it's over." Carl stepped more clearly into Toni's range of vision. He was at least four inches shorter than Nick and sported some excess flesh that wouldn't dare attach itself to Nick's body. His face was shadowed with beard, and his black hair grew in a horseshoe pattern around a bald center. When he looked at Nick again, she saw the resignation in his face.

"So the cops get a truckload of smack, we get shot at, and Lou gets fucked," Carl said. "Sounds good. You think you can manage to get in on this? I mean, you can't just show up—"

Nick held up a hand. "If I work this right, it'll be Lou's idea to send me along." He slapped Carl's back. "Get yourself a vest and wear it."

"I'll just borrow one from you. That way I'll be

covered clear to my knees."

Toni closed the door soundlessly when they returned to the living room. She crept back to bed in case Nick should check. She'd heard only a minute's worth of their conversation, but it was enough. More than enough. Nick had lost his brother to drugs and he'd wanted to kill Lou Taranto for that. He couldn't possibly be working for the biggest heroin supplier in the state. It just wasn't possible. He had to be one of the good guys.

She'd heard enough to know that there was a tight bond between the two men, and more than she wanted to know about what was going on tomorrow night. They were going to walk into a situation that could get them both killed.

She spent the remainder of the night awake, turning their words over and over in her mind.

In the morning, when she rose and showered and dressed, it wouldn't leave her alone. The image of bullets flying toward Nick—toward both of them— haunted her constantly.

He wasn't there when she walked into the living room. Did the man ever sleep? She dragged herself into the kitchen for some coffee, following the rich aroma that had reached her the second she'd opened the bedroom door. It smelled great, but the way her stomach was churning, she wondered if she could even handle a single cup. She filled a heavy stoneware mug despite her doubts and held it with both hands as she paced the room.

She shouldn't be wondering where Nick had gone

this morning. She shouldn't worry that he was already embroiled in a film noir-style gunfight.

Yeah, she shouldn't be worried but she was. She took the remote and checked the mansion, but she'd already known she wouldn't find him. A sense of emptiness pervaded the place with his absence.

God, what if he'd already gone on this suicide mission of his?

No. She'd heard them say that whatever was happening would happen tonight.

But would he return before all of that? Was he somewhere right now, preparing for it? Would he go directly to that hell of crisscrossing bullets?

She stood still, closed her eyes and took a bracing gulp of hot coffee, then grimaced. She hadn't put cream or sugar in it.

"Enough, already." She moved purposefully to the counter and spooned sugar into her mug, then stirred. To keep from imagining all sorts of melodramatic nonsense she could do nothing about, she decided to distract herself by writing.

An hour later the coffee was stone-cold and her mind was nowhere near Katrina Chekov's world. Her efforts ended when she tore a sheet from the notebook, crumpled it into a tight ball and threw it across the room. The pencil followed, as soon as she'd snapped it in half. The entire notebook sailed through the air a moment later to join its companions in a corner. Toni got to her feet and paced the room. The confinement made her claustrophobic. The knowledge that the door was sealed and that the only person who knew how to open it might get himself killed before he came back here to let her out had her chewing her nails. Sitting here doing nothing, while he might be out there getting shot at, had her crazy.

She stopped pacing when her agitated gait took her right up to the door. Her gaze fixed on the numbered panel beside it, and a new thought made itself heard above all the others.

The panel had ten numbered squares. She was fairly certain it took three to open the door. But which three? Did it matter? She'd have to hit on it eventually. She began with 1-1-1.

Nick had phoned Lou at the crack of dawn and arranged to meet with him at a truck stop off the highway. Always on time, Lou was waiting in a booth near the back of the place when Nick arrived.

He stood, clapped a hand to Nick's shoulder and waved him to the padded bench seat. Lou let his gaze sweep the place when they were both sitting, and Nick followed suit. There was a long counter facing the doors, and a line of stools with deep red upholstered seats. An old-fashioned cash register sat on one end of the counter, and a man who looked as if he ought to be in a boxing ring moved back and forth behind it. Booths like the one they were in lined the other three walls. The open floor was a maze of stackable shelving, all of it cluttered with snack foods, magazines and toiletries. The air was thick with the smell of hot grease.

"Nice place you picked, Nicky." Lou couldn't keep the worry from his voice. "What's wrong? Why'd you call so early?"

Nick sighed and tried to look tormented. He glanced at the waitress, whose parents had done a disservice by not getting her braces when she was young. She hurried toward them, pulling a pad from her apron pocket and a pen from her nest of brown hair. "Coffee," Nick told her. "You want some breakfast, Lou? It's on me."

Lou shook his head once. "I'm on a tight schedule."

"Just coffee, then," Nick told the girl. "Bring the pot."

She nodded, replaced the pad and was back in less than a minute with a bubble-shaped carafe. She turned over both their cups, filled them and disappeared again, seeming to sense that the two men did not want to be bothered.

Lou sipped. "Just cause I'm backing you to be made, Nick, that doesn't mean I'm at your beck and call. I came this time, but you need to know—"

"I know. It won't happen again, Lou."

Nodding once, Lou waited. Nick cleared his throat. "I've been thinking about what Vi—" He broke off, glancing around the place with feigned nervousness. "What our friend had to say the other day."

"He said a lot of things."

"About the vote," Nick clarified. "I'm afraid he

might've been right. I'm not proven."

"You took the broad out, Nicky. That's proof enough for me."

"You only have one vote."

Nick watched Lou's expression gradually go grim. Finally the fat man nodded, causing his flabby jowls to sway slightly. "Truth is, Nicky, the other bosses aren't sure about you yet. It might not go the way I wanted it to. But I'll keep backing you. Sooner or later—"

"I don't want it sooner or later, I want it now!" Nick made a show of forcing his temper back down. "Look, can't you set me up with something, give me some kind of assignment that would show my loyalty?"

Lou frowned and squeezed his chin in one hand. "There's nothing big enough going on—"

"Then it's hopeless." Nick leaned back hard and stared into his coffee cup.

Lou released his chin and drummed his fingers on the table. "There *is* a shipment coming in tonight. Not a big enough deal to earn you much clout—then again, it can't hurt."

Nick brought his head up fast. "I'll take anything you can give me, Lou. I want this so bad I can taste it."

He tried not to grin as Lou began to tell him about the shipment that would arrive by truck at his warehouse that night, and he whistled as he drove back to the mansion a little while later. This thing was going smoother than he'd hoped.

Toni was all the way up to the possible combinations beginning with 3 before she realized she'd made a big mistake. 3-1-1 had no effect on the security system. When she tried 3-1-2, a bell started ringing—a high-pitched jangling that refused to stop stabbed at her ears and pierced her brain. The red lights beside the numbered panel flashed at her like scolding eyes.

She jumped back, barely suppressing a yelp when the door flew open and Nick's broad frame filled her vision. His face taut with anger, he stepped inside, slammed the door and rapidly punched a series of numbers on the panel. The alarm died at once, leaving a leaden silence in its place.

"What kind of asinine stunt was that?" He didn't raise his voice, but each clipped word made his displeasure perfectly clear.

She was so relieved to see him back in one piece that his ill humor didn't faze her. She turned her back to him so he wouldn't see it in her face, still trying to convince herself that her gnawing worry had been for her own sake, not his. If something happened to Nick, she'd be imprisoned here indefinitely. She hadn't truly cared that he might get shot—or killed. She wouldn't let herself care. She didn't even know who the real Nick Manelli was.

"Well?"

She pressed her fingertips to her temples and closed her eyes. "I...had to try."

"Why, for God's sake? Toni, you're safe here. You wouldn't be out there. I thought you understood that."

She turned to face him, feeling a bristle of anger that chased away her limp relief. "You can't expect me to sit here, docile as a lamb, while life-and-death decisions are being made for me by a man I'm not even sure I can trust!"

His brows came together. "*Not sure* you can trust? Isn't that a major change in attitude? I thought you had me pegged as a rung or two below Satan."

She averted her gaze and shrugged.

"As for sitting here, docile as a lamb, that's the last thing I expect from you, lady. 'Docile' is not an adjective I'd use to describe you. But you are here and you are going to stay so you might as well resign yourself to the fact. This place is buttoned up tighter than a spinster's corset. You're here until I say otherwise."

To Toni's ears it was a challenge. "Is that so? Well, I guess that's right. I'm here and I've got nothing but time on my hands. If I can't find a way out of this hole, then my name isn't Toni Ri—" She stopped herself just before she blurted "Rio."

Nick's eyes narrowed and he studied her face. His gaze swept the room, falling on the crumpled paper and abused notebook in the corner. She shook her head and spun away to pace to the kitchen. He drew a long breath and let it out slowly. "Confinement's making you crazy, huh?"

She turned, then dropped her gaze before his,

because he seemed to see so much. It was making her a lot more crazy since she'd overheard that conversation last night.

"Sit down, Toni."

She didn't argue. She was too tired. She went to the sofa and curled on one end with her legs tucked beneath her. Imagining him caught in the cross fire, cops firing at him from one side, criminals from the other, had taken a lot of energy. The relief left her weak. Nick sat down close to her. She felt his lingering gaze but didn't return it. She braced her elbow on the cushioned arm and rested her forehead in her upturned palm.

"I need you to promise not to mess with the security system again, Toni. I can't have the alarm going off every time I leave the house."

"I don't believe this," she murmured. "My life's turned inside out, my sister probably thinks I'm dead, and you're worried about your precious security system?"

He dropped his gaze and seemed to consider his next words carefully before speaking. Finally he looked at her again. "For all I know, the house could be wired. Do you know what that means?"

Toni's curiosity rose to the surface like a shark at the scent of blood. It swallowed her frustration in one bite, her anger in the next. "Wired by whom? The police?"

He looked away. "Maybe."

"No," she said softly. "It's Taranto, isn't it? You think Taranto might be listening in." She knew she was right because the slight flicker in his eyes gave him away.

"The point is, those alarms would seem curious to *anyone* who might be eavesdropping. What if it was Taranto? If he finds out you're here…"

He didn't finish. He didn't have to. Toni was well aware what her fate would be if Taranto discovered her. That Nick thought Taranto would trust him so little—that was interesting to her.

"Why don't you just sweep the house?" She asked the question only to prolong the conversation. She'd hoped he'd say something that would confirm her suspicion that he was not what he pretended.

He watched her as he spoke. "The house is too big to sweep daily. I'd miss some nook or cranny."

Unconsciously chewing her thumbnail, Toni looked up suddenly. "*That's* why you stay in this apartment. It's small, easy to sweep, and no one knows it's here so it's unlikely they'd bug it anyway." She paused, looking around the room with new understanding. "The phone must be secure, too. Probably has a bug signal, doesn't it? What if someone tries to trace a call? Does it bounce off relays and give them some sham number in Brooklyn or something?"

He stared at her for a long moment. "You seem to know a lot about this stuff, Toni. You want to tell me why that is?"

She'd allowed herself to get caught up in her own excitement and had run off at the mouth, she realized grimly. She tried to look nonchalant and shrugged. If he was a cop, she must be making him hellishly uncomfortable. If not, she might very well have put herself at risk. "I read a lot of thrillers."

His jaw was tight, and his brown eyes probed hers like surgical instruments. "Then you ought to be able to see why it would be a big mistake to mess with the panel again. That alarm going off when I'm not even in the house is as good as a flare going up on a dark night. The wrong people notice it, it will be as bad for you as it will be for me." His tone was calmly dictatorial—as if he expected no disagreement on her part. As if he would not tolerate any disagreement.

He had a way of putting things so they made perfect sense, even in this crazy situation. She found herself feeling guilty for setting off the alarm. "I'll promise not to try it again if you'll stop disappearing without a word. I was wor— I was scared when I got up this morning and you were gone. What was I supposed to do? I wasn't even sure you'd be back. I couldn't just sit in front of the television and wait for a news report to tell me your body had been found in a swamp somewhere—"

"What the hell are you talking about?" He shook his head, puzzled. Then understanding crept over his face. "You were listening last night."

"Not long enough," she shot back. She was tired of playing games with him. "I didn't hear a word to explain why two seemingly sane men would deliberately put themselves into the middle of a shooting match."

He caught her chin and tilted it up so he could

stare down into her eyes. She hoped to God he couldn't see what caused the intense burning behind them. "Don't tell me you were worried about me."

She jerked her chin free, angry because she had been, no matter how much she wanted to deny it. "Dream on, Manelli."

"I will if you will, del Rio."

He referred to her dream last night, of course. She could have slapped him for that remark. She couldn't help it if her subconscious mind was unstable enough to conjure images of him, of them...

She shook her head and pretended she didn't know what he was talking about. "I just don't care to be left in the cell when the jailer checks out." She glanced at him again, sensing a chance to get a clue to the truth from him. "Why would you risk your life for Lou Taranto? Don't you realize he is personally responsible for seventy percent of the heroin in the city?" She shook her head. "I would think that when you lost your own brother to that garbage you'd—"

"You *are* a good listener, aren't you?" He kept a tight hold on his anger, but she could see it there. It flashed in those deep brown eyes. "My brother is none of your business." His gaze wavered. He looked at his hands. "He's dead and buried. He has nothing to do with me or what I choose to do with my life."

The raw agony in his voice was like a whip lashing her heart. It also gave the lie away. His brother had everything to do with his life. She couldn't stop her hand from going to his arm. "That was hitting below the belt. I'm sorry." He didn't look at her. "Nick?"

"Go change," he told her. "I'll take you down to the gym for an hour."

All day Nick tried to shake the feeling of impending doom. The damn woman was hiding something from him; he was sure of it. She knew about bugs and sweeping for them. She knew about phone taps and bug signals. Worse than that, he was sure she suspected his *goodfella* routine was a sham. She wouldn't let it drop. She was like a dog with a three-day-old bone. She had to keep gnawing at it.

And the ways she had of getting at him! When she looked at him with those giant, dark-jewel eyes, he wanted to tell her everything. When she'd mentioned his brother, he nearly had. To let her think he could work for Danny's killer was too much—but he had to do it.

He'd left her alone in the gym for over an hour. When he'd finally interrupted, she was doing transverse sit-ups on an incline bench. For a moment he just watched her. Her face was red. Her hair was damp and sticking to her face. The T-shirt she wore had wet spots beneath her breasts and between them, and in the middle of her back.

He felt bad for having kept her cooped up the way he had and he tried to make up for it. He took her swimming, then served her lunch in the formal dining room, warning her first they'd have to remain quiet. He took her on a tour of the entire mansion and found himself enjoying it, although neither of them could speak above a whisper.

The day passed quickly, and they were back in the hidden apartment now. She was soaking in a hot bath to ease her muscles after the workout she'd inflicted on herself. While she was occupied, Nick plugged in the phone and dialed his supervisor's number. He needed to know what the background check on Toni had turned up. He was told that Harry was "unavailable." He could be reached later tonight, but then Nick would be unavailable. He'd have to wait until tomorrow.

Toni emerged from her bath with all that wild black hair, still damp, pulled back in a ponytail. She wore a pair of baggy gray sweats and a matching pullover with Yosemite Sam on the front. How was it possible, he heard himself wonder, for a woman to look so alluring with Yosemite Sam on her chest?

"What's the matter? Do I have something caught between my teeth?"

Nick shook himself. "What?"

"You were staring," she told him. She moved through the living room, into the kitchen, and yanked open the refrigerator. She took out a can of cola, popped the top and took a long drink. Nick watched her throat move as she swallowed. He had to force his gaze away from her.

When he glanced up again, she was the one staring. Her eyes were focused on a point just beyond him, and her face was slightly pale. He turned to see what had caught her attention. The bulletproof vest he'd dug out was slung over the back of the couch. She looked at it as if she thought it might come to life and bite her.

"You're really going to do this, aren't you?"

"I don't have a choice, Toni, and if it's all the same to you, I'd just as soon not spend the next hour and a half talking about it."

She blinked fast and averted her face. "You could get yourself killed—"

"Only if you pray real hard."

Her head snapped around, her eyes hard as coal chips. "I wouldn't pray for that. You don't really think I could, do you?"

"I was kidding. Lighten up, will you?" He stepped closer to her. "Look, I'd rather think about something else until it's time to go."

Her eyes got all smoky and dark as they latched onto his.

He pointed to the box on the coffee table. "I was referring to that. Of course, if you'd rather—"

"A jigsaw puzzle?" Toni frowned and went to the table, picking up the colorful box and shaking it so the pieces rattled. "You're ready to walk into a shooting gallery disguised as a duck, and you want to put a jigsaw puzzle together?"

"It's a ritual." Nick shrugged. He took the box from her and dumped the pieces in a chaotic mound on the carpet. "Helps me focus."

He didn't mention that it would also—he hoped— help him keep his mind away from the thought that had been recurring all day: that if he was going to die tonight, and if he'd been given a last request, it would have been to spend several hours in bed with Antonia. Visions of her small, firm body, unclothed and crushed against his, crept into his mind unbidden. Whenever he touched her or caught the barest hint of her scent, he had to restrain himself from taking her into his arms and kissing her breath away. When had this obsession with her taken over? He was about to go into battle, for God's sake—yet all he could think about was how it would feel to love every inch of the ebony-eyed beauty.

He sat cross-legged on the floor and began sorting the outside pieces, forcing himself to concentrate on the task at hand.

Toni stopped arguing the sanity of doing a puzzle at a time like this as soon as she thought about how nervous he must be. She tried to imagine how she would feel if she knew that in a short time people would be shooting at her. She'd go along with the puzzle thing, she decided, if it would help Nick not to think about what was ahead of him tonight.

Nick's intense concentration made a furrow between his brows Toni ignored the urge to put her finger there to smooth it away.

"I probably had a hundred jigsaws when I was a kid," he said softly.

"I had a couple," she responded. "But my favorite

pastime was paint-by-numbers. You remember those black velvet ones? Took forever to dry, but they were so pretty they were worth the wait."

He glanced up at her, and his relaxed smile took her breath away. "I'll bet it killed you—the waiting."

"Drove me crazy! I could only do one color, then wait and wait for it to dry before I could do another. I used to prop the picture on a chair and point an electric fan at it."

"Wouldn't a hair dryer have been faster?"

"Who has patience enough to stand around holding a hair dryer for hours on end?"

"Not you, that's for sure." He held her gaze with his, then looked down again and fit a corner piece to another. "When did you start writing?"

"I don't know exactly. It's just something I've always done. First it was journals and silly poetry and fairy tales. It wasn't until high school that I got into the serious stuff."

He looked up again, his gaze intense. "Such as?"

She frowned for a moment before deciding it wouldn't hurt to be honest with him. To a point, anyway. "Social injustice, corruption, that kind of thing." She wondered if he would get bored with the subject. He leaned forward, the puzzle momentarily forgotten.

"Okay, so what was the first so-called serious thing you wrote about?"

"Prejudice."

She didn't elaborate. Nick studied her. "Tell me about it."

Toni looked at him. She hadn't talked about it in a very long time. It was a painful subject. In her entire life, the only person who'd been allowed to glimpse just how painful, had been her mother. And even she had never known the extent of Toni's guilt. She was struck all at once with the urge to share it with someone—with Nick.

She cleared her throat, set down the puzzle piece she'd been trying to fit. "It was during my senior year—a nurse was raped and murdered, her body found in the hospital parking lot. There were no witnesses, no fingerprints. No DNA sample. But they managed to get a blood type."

She couldn't go on with his eyes focused unblinkingly on hers, so she got up and walked a few steps away. "The only clue was a tie clip found at the scene. It was one of three that had been awarded to three of the hospital's outstanding surgeons something like twelve years earlier."

"That must have narrowed it down," Nick said. He sounded puzzled, and in a moment she heard him get to his feet, as well. "Did you know the woman?"

She shook her head. "No."

"One of the suspects, then?"

She nodded. "My father."

She heard Nick suck in his breath, but hurried to continue before he could say something that would make her change her mind. "None of the surgeons were able to produce their tie clips. It had been twelve years, after all. They all had alibis for the time of the murder, but people lie, so none were rock solid. My father was home that night. I know because I was home that night, too."

She glanced at Nick and found him frowning. "What happened?"

"The other two were Caucasian," she said softly. "My father was one hundred percent Puerto Rican. What do you think happened?"

Nick shook his head. "The blood type—"

"Could have been any one of them."

"But they didn't convict him—not with evidence that flimsy."

"No," she told him. "It never went to trial. But during the investigation, Dad's...indiscretions came out. He'd had affairs. He'd fathered at least three other children by three other women. For sure. There was evidence there could be more. My sister, the one I've mentioned, she's one of them. The only one I've managed to make contact with. I've never even met the others. We don't even know who they are."

"Your poor mother."

She nodded. "I saw what was happening. Dad was ostracized. The hospital suspended him. He was shunned by the community. Even my mother turned against him."

"Given all the other women, maybe you can't blame her."

"I don't. I never did. I just thought she could've dealt with it after. A murder charge trumps a string of affairs, you know?" She lowered her head, remembering how angry she'd been at her mom, still not sure she could've had any other reaction. "We started getting hate mail and crank calls. He was dying inside. I could see it happening right in front of me and I wouldn't admit it. I just kept thinking everything would be all right. Then the day came. The last day. He kissed me goodbye..." She looked up, into Nick's eyes.

Nick stood close to her, put his hands on her shoulders, gave them a comforting squeeze. "Where did he go?"

She clenched her jaw, but forced herself to relax it and tell him the rest. She'd come this far. For some reason she was compelled to let Nick know he wasn't the only one with trauma in his childhood. "They found his car at the bottom of a ravine. It was ruled an accident. But it wasn't. I knew it wasn't. The thing is, I knew it before he left, but I wouldn't believe it." In her life she'd never uttered the confession to anyone else. It had been eating at her soul for thirteen years. "I could have stopped him, Nick. I could have told my mother or the police or someone. But I didn't have the courage to do it."

He pulled her into his arms and held her to him. "It's okay, cry."

She did, letting the hot tears soak into his shirt and absorbing his strength. "This is stupid. I'm not a little girl anymore." She sniffed and tried to straighten.

He looked at her, shook his head. "You've been living with a heap of guilt, Toni. It had to come out sometime. It wasn't your fault. You might have seen the signs afterward, but hindsight is always clearer."

"I should have stopped him," she repeated. "God only knows why I'm telling you all this."

"Maybe for the same reason I told you about my family," he said slowly.

"Maybe," she whispered. She thought it might be the most honest moment that had passed between them since their first encounter. She blinked her eyes dry and cleared her throat, allowing the pain to slip away into the past where it belonged. "When my grief subsided enough to vent some of the anger, I wrote a lot. Scathing editorials about prejudiced bigots who see everything according to its color, or judge people by their past mistakes. My focus broadened gradually, until I was writing about anything I saw as unjust and exposing those responsible."

Nick nodded and then his eyes narrowed. "Is that what you were doing in the alley?"

She was surprised by his insight. She hadn't intended to give herself away by revealing some of her past. Her face must have confirmed his suspicion because he let the arms that had been so comforting, fall to his sides. "Tell me the truth, Toni," he said slowly. "Don't keep secrets that could get us both killed. Not today."

She looked at him for a long time and then at the floor. "You want the truth? Truth is, I'm some kind of fool, Nick. Truth is, I'm getting used to having you around and I'd really hate to see you riddled with bullet holes. So much so that I'm willing to tell you all of it... if you'll call this off." She put a palm to his cheek and stared hard into his eyes. "I don't want you to go."

He swallowed hard. She saw his Adam's apple move. His hands flattened themselves to her cheeks, and he tipped her face up, searching it with his eyes. She felt his warm breath on her lips. When his lips parted, she thought he would kiss her. Instead, he said, "Then there *is* something you're not telling me."

Disappointment rinsed through her. His eyes had been so intense—but she banished that thought. "No more than what you're not telling me." She would have pulled her face from his hands, but the look on his paralyzed her. For an instant she glimpsed pain and raw longing. Then his lips came down to meet hers, and she couldn't help but stand on tiptoe to meet them halfway. He kissed her softly, parting his lips to capture hers between them and sipping at them like he would a fine wine.

Toni's knees trembled. Her heart fluttered in her chest, and before she'd made a conscious decision to do so, her hands had slipped down to link around his neck. Her body melded to his. Her lips relaxed open at the first gentle nudging of his tongue. She welcomed it.

Nick's hands left her face to cradle her head. His fingers tangled in her hair. His stroking tongue set her on fire, and the subtle movements of his hips told her that he was just as aroused. When he lifted his mouth away, she pulled him in again, kissed him again. With a low groan, he complied with her unspoken request and kissed her once more. He kissed her until her breathing was broken and ragged, until her head was spinning and her entire body throbbed with wanting him.

Finally he straightened and held her to him. Her head rested against his chest. His heart hammered like a drum. He was breathing as erratically as she was. His voice was barely more than a whisper when he spoke. "You're seeing things that aren't there."

She frowned and would have looked up, but he held her where she was.

"You'd rather believe a fairy tale than to admit the truth, Toni," he went on. "I'm not hiding a damn thing. I'm exactly what I seem. Your problem is you can't stand to admit that you're hot for Lou Taranto's right-hand man."

Toni stiffened, and this time he let her step away from him. He turned his back on her, picked up the vest and put it on. His words were like knives in her heart— mostly, she realized, because they were true.

"You want to pick up where we left off when I get back, I'll be happy to cooperate," he said. "But you need to know who I am." He slammed a clip into his gun with the heel of his hand and worked the action. He never even looked at her. "Right now I have to go. Lou's counting on me."

CHAPTER 6

Toni's face burned with humiliation as she stared at the door he'd just slammed. She'd made a fool of herself, let herself believe in something that was pure fantasy. Like a little girl dreaming of a knight in shining armor, she'd allowed her imagination to twist the truth. She'd seen everything exactly the way she'd wanted to see it. Nick had nailed the reason, in his crude way. She couldn't allow herself to feel what she was feeling for a criminal, so she'd built him into a hero.

"How could I have been such an idiot?" She turned from the door, and her gaze darted around the empty room, not really seeing anything. "My God, I almost told him..." She bit her lip, unwilling to complete the thought aloud. Hadn't he just warned her about listening devices that might be in the house? Who was to say he hadn't planted a few of his own right here? She'd come perilously close to admitting her alter ego tonight. She'd almost told him she was Toni Rio. If he truly worked for Taranto, that would be suicide.

She grimaced when she realized she'd mentally injected an *if* into the thought. Was she still determined to think he was some kind of a saint? Her eyes burned and a stabbing sense of betrayal twisted inside, even deeper than the humiliation. It made no sense, that feeling. He'd never claimed to be anything but what he was. Yet she'd told him her most painful secrets. She'd bared her heart's deepest wounds to him.

He'd seemed to care, she thought miserably. The way he held her and spoke softly....

So what? Even a morally bankrupt bastard was entitled to noble impulses now and then.

What about all the other things that don't fit? What about all the surveillance equipment, and his fear of being monitored by Taranto? Why the hidden apartment—the traveling telephone—the late-night meetings with Carl?

More than that, her mind whispered. There was his brother, who'd died of a drug overdose. Just the mention of his brother brought Nick extreme pain. How could he be working for Taranto?

Angry with herself for trying to make a case for her own wishful thinking, she wondered if her theory that he was a cop might still be valid. She was too close to this to be sure. It was like a work in progress at the moment, like the jigsaw puzzle on the floor. She wouldn't be able to look at things objectively until she was able to distance herself.

The fact was, she'd allowed herself to begin to care about Nick. The lines between realistic theory and whimsical fantasy had blurred until she couldn't distinguish one from the other. She had to get the hell out of here. Tonight.

Before she let herself forget his cruel words and started seeing him as a character from one of her books.

She paused as she realized that was exactly what she'd been doing. Nick was exactly the type Katrina would go for. Built like Atlas, arrogant and dangerous—that air of mystery about him.

But she was not Katrina Chekov, she reminded herself. The things she'd seen in him had been different. His inability to hurt her or even let her go hungry. That well-hidden gentleness that wasn't nearly as well hidden as he thought. And while she'd exposed her secret pain to him, she remembered that she'd seen his, as well. The pain of being abandoned by his parents and of losing his brother, the pain he pretended didn't hurt at all.

Toni shook her head slowly. No, she couldn't stay here another night. She had to leave before she did something she might regret for the rest of her life.

An hour later, on an elevated loading dock outside the warehouse with a handful of Taranto's lower level thugs, Nick was still replaying that encounter in his head. He'd only glimpsed the hurt in Toni's eyes briefly before he'd looked away. If he faced her, he was sure she'd see right through his act. He wanted to tell her the truth so bad it was eating him up from the inside out. But he couldn't. Taranto was an expert at getting the truth out of people. He was damn good, too, at sensing when a person had something to tell or when they honestly knew nothing. If he ever got his filthy hands on Toni, it would be far better for her if she fell into the latter category.

Damn, the effect that woman had on him was like wildfire on a tinder-dry forest. He could still taste her on his lips, feel her small body straining against him. Every move she made, every breath that mingled with his had been a plea. *Tell me. Trust me.*

Trust her. He couldn't do that, dammit. Trusting other people had never brought him anything but disappointment. He'd be stupid to trust her when he knew she was hiding something. She had her own agenda. Who was to say she wouldn't get whatever information she could from him and then just walk away? And why the hell shouldn't she? Everyone he'd ever cared for had. He'd learned to depend on no one but himself. Leaning on others brought nothing but pain. It made you weak, vulnerable.

Since Danny's death, the grand finale in a series of desertions, Nick had existed in a virtual vacuum. No one got close to him. When he needed sexual release, he found it with strangers. He rarely even asked their names. His encounters with women were always cold, preplanned exchanges. He was consistently sober, consistently protected and never really satisfied.

The only one to breach his self-imposed seclusion was Carl. But Carl had been close to him before his mother had walked out, before his father had been caught running from that liquor store with a six-pack, a wad of money and a loaded gun, and before Danny had died. In all that time, Carl had never broken faith. He'd always been there. But even with that, Nick lived with the constant certainty that Carl, too, would disappear one day. He tried not to need his best friend. People never abandoned you when you were aloof. As long as you could take them or leave them, they tended to hang around. The minute you needed them, they vanished like a magician's trick. *Poof! You're on your own again, pal.*

"Here it is." Carl's voice shook him out of his brooding thoughts.

Nick watched the red taillights come closer as the semi backed up to the loading dock. The only other light was from a single bulb overhead, just enough so they could see what they were doing inside the warehouse. Besides Nick and Carl, three others waited to help unload the shipment.

Rosco, an old faithful employee of Lou's who'd never had the ambition to move up through the ranks, stood a few feet away, an automatic rifle gripped in a two-handed, ready-to-fire, hold. He was the lookout. The other two were younger, barely out of their teens, but already loyal lackeys to Lou's machine. One called himself Sly, the other, Jake. Nick figured their real names were something like

Howard and Irving.

When the truck came to a halt, Nick went outside and lifted the lever to release the trailer's rear doors. He swung them open and glanced inside. The crates looked for all the world like an innocent cargo of coffee. The heroin was buried in the fragrant beans, whose aroma would usually throw drug-sniffing dogs off the scent.

The two kids rushed past him into the trailer, grabbed a crate each and moved them onto a waiting pallet. Carl pulled out onto the loading dock with a forklift. When the pallet was filled, he would pick it up on the tines and take it inside the warehouse. Nick glanced out into the darkness. Somewhere out there police officers must be waiting. Any second the night could explode with muzzle flashes and lethal bullets. Still his mind kept wandering into the zone he'd deemed forbidden. He was thinking of Toni, wondering if his cruel words had caused her any tears. She'd had enough pain in her life. Damn woman was systematically chipping away at the walls he'd so painstakingly erected...and that scared him.

When a spotlight blinded him, Nick jerked in surprise, even though he'd known it would come sooner or later. A bullhorn-enhanced voice drilled through the white glare. "This is the police. Step away from the truck, keeping your hands—"

And then Taranto's men started shooting. The kids dove for cover, dropping crates and pulling their guns. Coffee beans spilled all over the place. Rosco squeezed off a rapid burst of fire. The cops shot back without missing a beat, and Nick knew that the men on the dock, himself included, were sitting ducks. He glanced around for decent cover, saw Jake and Sly crouching behind an upturned crate, which was no cover at all. The spotlight moved, bathed them.

Nick charged across the dock, slamming into the two kids and knocking them to the ground five feet below. He almost went over the edge himself, but managed not to. Looking behind him, he saw Rosco lying on the platform. He wasn't moving. He must've been hit in the first volley. Nick lunged toward him and grabbed the AK rifle he'd dropped, pointed it, squeezed the trigger and held, straining to keep the barrel from lifting skyward with the force of the recoil until he'd put the spotlight out.

Carl, where the hell was Carl?

Nick found him, crouching behind the forklift. Before he could move closer, Carl pulled his handgun and shot the light bulb that was dangling over his head, plunging them into total darkness. Nick made his way toward him, bullets flying around him like a rainstorm. At least they had the benefit of darkness now. He and Carl crouched low, ran to the edge and jumped over it, joining the two younger guys on the gravel-covered ground.

A searing pain in his left thigh drew Nick's hand to it. It came away warm and moist. With the adrenaline pumping, he hadn't even felt the bullet rip into him, but he sure as hell felt it now. The two kids were still firing back at the cops, but Nick knew they couldn't see enough to hit any of them. "Knock it off, guys, you're just showing 'em where we are." He clasped Carl's shoulder. "We've got to try for the car. They won't wait long to move in." The unspoken conclusion to the sentence was in his friend's eyes. *And then one of these crazy punks might kill some of them.*

Carl nodded, nudged the other two, and the four of them ran for the nearest vehicle. Nick had left his car close and behind a steel storage pod for this very reason. They had a precarious three-second start before the police realized what had happened. Nick slid into the passenger seat, and Carl took the wheel as the two kids dove into the backseat. Carl slammed the shift into Drive and the pedal to the floor, sending a shower of loose stones behind them. Seconds later, screaming sirens came to life.

Nick glanced over his shoulder at the two in the back seat. "You two all right?"

"Yeah," Sly replied. "Damn, I thought we were all goners! I could feel the freakin' bullets flyin' past me. I could *feel* 'em. Damn!"

Jake said nothing. He sat still, his eyes dilated and his skin pale in the dim interior of the car. Nick had a feeling he'd think twice before he decided to devote his remaining years to working for Lou Taranto.

Carl's stream of fluent cursing brought Nick's head around. "You're bleeding, Nick. You're hit."

"Just drive," Nick told him. "It's nothing." He looked down now and saw that his pant leg was soaked in blood. The warm trickle along his outer thigh told him it was still flowing. He slipped the belt from his waist, wrapped it around the wounded thigh, just above the injury, and pulled it tight.

Carl rounded a corner, tires squealing, and came to a rubber-burning stop. "Out, you two," he ordered the boys in the back. "Stay out of sight for an hour, then get your butts home." The two tumbled out the same door and vanished into a vacant building just as Carl pulled away from the curb.

"I'm taking you to a hospital Nick. You're bleeding like—"

"Forget it!" Nick yanked the belt tighter and held it mercilessly. "It's stopping. They catch up with us, and we'll be tied up for God knows how long. I can't leave Toni to her own devices for more than a few of hours. You don't know what kind of hell she'd raise."

"What damage can she do? She's under lock and key."

"You don't know her."

Toni's plan was simple. Nick would open the door, she would give him a healthy dose of hair spray in the face and run like hell. She'd wrapped a change of clothes and her notebook in one of his spare blankets, since there was no telling how long it would take her to find help. The bundle rested close enough so she could grab it as she fled. She watched for his car on the monitor, sighing her relief when it finally pulled up at the gate. Thank God. She'd started to think something might really have happened to him.

Flicking off the TV, she tossed the remote over the row of books on the shelf. In case her escape attempt failed, no point letting on that she knew about the monitor. She positioned herself near the door, lifted the hair-spray can and waited.

It seemed to take an unreasonably long time for him to come upstairs. She grew restless. Her feet itched and she shifted her weight back and forth from one to the other.

Finally the door moved and Toni braced herself. It opened. Her finger touched the knob on the top of the can. Carl came through with Nick's arm anchored over his shoulders. Nick's head was bowed.

Toni saw the scarlet blood dripping from his pant leg. His head came up. He met her horrified stare, and she could see the pain on his face. The hairspray can fell to the floor, forgotten in her rush to pull his free arm around her and help Carl get him inside. "To the bedroom," she instructed, and she and Carl half carried Nick there and clumsily eased his huge body onto the edge of the bed. She released him long enough to tear the covers back, then grabbed him again and eased him down onto the bed.

"What the hell happened?" She tried not to look at Nick's face, at the pallor of his skin, and the lines etched at the corners of his mouth. Hooking a finger into what she presumed to be a bullet hole in his pant leg, just below the belt he'd twisted around his thigh, she tore the fabric wider.

"It's nothing. A graze," Nick ground out. He wasn't lying flat, but holding his head and shoulders off the bed. She could hear the effort he made to keep his voice normal, and the way he struggled to breathe deeply and regularly. The man couldn't admit to weakness at all, even with a quart of blood soaking his clothes. He was infuriating.

"He was shot," Carl finally answered.

She realized it had been a stupid question. Of course he'd been shot, what else? A mottled chasm in his flesh still pulsed blood. She couldn't see the wound well until she cleaned some of the blood away.

Her gaze pinned Carl. "Prop his feet on pillows— they ought to be elevated. Get the wounded leg higher. It'll slow the bleeding." She got off the bed. "Take his shoes off, too."

Carl's quick nod assured her he'd do what she asked. She ran into the bathroom, dug into the medicine cabinet and gathered everything she thought might be of use: gauze pads and a roll of gauze, a tube of antiseptic ointment, some Ibuprofen tablets, adhesive tape. She carried all of it into the bedroom, dumped it on the nightstand, then rushed back for a basin of warm water, a washcloth and a bar of soap.

She was faster than Carl—then again, the poor man was shaking so hard it was amazing he could stay upright himself. She hurried into the kitchen for the bottle of whiskey she'd found there before and a small glass. As she headed back, she glanced out the wide-open bookcase door. A little shudder passed through her. Could the one who'd shot Nick have followed them? She closed the door and raced back to the bedside.

She had to swallow hard before she could speak. All of this was almost too much. Seeing that much blood, knowing it was his... She twisted the cap from the whiskey bottle and poured with an amazingly steady hand. Leaning over him, she supported Nick's head and held the glass to his lips with the other.

"Hell, I'm not dying." He took the glass from her and swallowed the contents. Toni poured another shot as soon as he'd emptied the glass. She handed him some pain reliever to swallow with it this time.

"Will you quit with this, Toni? I'm all right."

"Shut up and drink." Fear for him made her voice sharp. "And then you can quit this macho bull and lie down. It's a strain to sit up and you know it."

Again Nick downed the whiskey. But he didn't lie down. Toni sat on the bed and tore the pant leg completely off. Then she began washing the blood away from his thigh. Carl had Nick's leg propped on four pillows, and had tightened the belt. The blood flow had slowed to a trickle.

"Carl, go close the door," Nick said, watching her, "before my bird decides to fly the coop."

She didn't pause in her removal of the blood with the wet, soapy cloth. "I already closed the door. I was afraid you might have been followed. Didn't want whoever did this to walk right in and finish the job." She dipped the cloth and squeezed, continued washing, repeated. God, there was a lot of blood.

"Your mistake," Nick said slowly. "I was shot by a cop. If he had followed me, he'd have been your ticket out."

"I figured that out all by myself," she replied. "And if I'd wanted out, Nick, I wouldn't be here. Don't kid yourself about that. I could've been out of here days ago if I wanted." She'd removed most of the blood by now. The bullet's path had dug a furrow along his outer thigh. He was lucky it hadn't been fractionally more to the right. It could've cost him his leg. She took the whiskey bottle and removed the cap again. "Another shot?"

He shook his head.

Toni took a folded towel and slid it beneath his thigh, then she tipped the bottle up and rinsed the wound in whiskey. She felt his body stiffen, heard the air he sucked through his teeth. Carl turned away, clapping a hand to his mouth.

Toni used a gauze pad to absorb the blood-colored whiskey that ran from the gash, down the sides of his leg, and prepared to pour a bit more over the wound. She glanced at Carl. In another minute he'd be puking. "You two must've left a blood trail right up to that cliché bookcase door. Maybe you ought to clean that up before your boss shows up to check on you."

"Yeah, right. I hadn't thought of..." He stopped and glanced at Nick. "If you guys don't need me."

"It's not as bad as it looks," Toni told him. "He'll be fine, and I can handle this alone."

Carl's relieved sigh filled the room. He sought Nick's nod before he turned and left them alone.

Toni rinsed the wound again, then began pulling

the edges together and taping them to hold them tight. "I know it hurts," she told him. "You ought to have stitches, but tape'll have to do. Just hold on and I'll get it over with as fast as I can. If you want another shot, for God's sake say so."

He said nothing. She finished closing the wound, coated it in ointment and then several pads, and then wrapped gauze around his entire thigh several times and taped it down.

He was still sitting up, and his expression was peculiar when she sat back again, and looked him in the eye. He seemed puzzled, as if he couldn't quite fathom what she was doing. She hoped he hadn't lost a lot more blood than she realized, as she slowly released the belt and watched the white gauze, waiting for—half expecting— a red stain to appear. It didn't.

"It will be okay," she said. "We'll have Carl get some more bandages and some antibiotics if he can manage it. You don't want to risk infect—" She stopped short when his hand shot out to encircle her wrist. He was staring intently, frowning, not angrily, when she looked up.

"The door was wide open, Toni. Why didn't you leave?"

She shook her head. "That has to be the stupidest question I've heard in a year."

"Not from where I stand. I saw the hair spray, the little pack you had ready. You were planning to run."

"That was before I knew you'd got yourself shot."

"What difference does it make?"

She looked at him and frowned. "I couldn't leave you like that. You needed me, for God's sake. You think I could just turn my back and walk out and leave you bleeding all over the floor?"

"Plenty of people have." He let his head fall back to the pillows.

Toni heard the double meaning behind the remark, and again she saw beyond the facade of toughness to the real hurt inside him. "Not me, Nick," she told him softly. "I don't walk out on people—not even when they deserve it." She got up and carried the basin of blood-tinted water into the bathroom to pour it down the sink and rinse it clean. She refilled it, grabbed a clean cloth and returned to the bed.

"You're talking about what I said to you before I left."

She nodded, trying not to feel again the hurt his words had inflicted.

Carl's voice from the doorway reminded Toni of his presence. "Bloodstains are all taken care of." His anxious eyes never left Nick's face. "I still think you should go to a hospital."

"I told you it's nothing."

"Yeah, well, I'm spending the night just to be sure."

"You can't do that, Carl. We're acquaintances, don't forget. We start acting like bosom buddies and—"

"I thought you two had known each other for years?" Toni's question brought a sudden wariness to both men's eyes. Nick's gaze held hers, tired but unwavering. Carl looked at her, then away, then back again.

"Maybe—uh—Nick and I ought to discuss this in private, if you don't mind, Miss—"

"It's Toni. I suppose you want me to believe you're another one of Taranto's hired killers? Shouldn't you just grab me by the hair, shove me through the door, call me a few choice names and threaten to kill me if you catch me listening? You probably don't realize it, but I've seen the way Taranto's men conduct their business. I don't believe the words 'If you don't mind, Miss' exist in their limited vocabulary."

"Don't ask her to leave, Carl. She'd just press her ear to the door anyway."

She glanced at Nick again. He sounded drained. He looked worse. Pale, shaky.

"I'm sorry," she said. "I'm stressed out. Look, if you want to talk, fine. But Nick, you really ought to rest. You lost a lot of blood—"

"Go home, Carl. I'll be fine."

"If it starts bleeding again, what're you gonna do?" Carl demanded. "The door's locked, you can't leave a phone in here. How could she even get help for you?"

Toni felt a shiver go through her. "He's right, Nick," she whispered.

"He can't stay." Nick's eyes looked puffy and leaden. He was obviously wrung out. He shouldn't waste his energy arguing. Still, Toni knew it would be stupid for her to stay alone with him, with no way to summon help in an emergency. Nick sighed loudly.

"Carl, punch the combination into the door before you pull it closed. That way the lock won't engage. If something happens, Toni can go downstairs and call an ambulance. Okay?"

"And if Lou's got the phone tapped?"

"I'll tell him it was just a hooker. He'll buy it. I know him."

Carl glanced uneasily at Toni. "And if she decides to take a walk?"

"I won't." She saw the doubt in Carl's eyes. "For God's sake, you guys are the ones claiming to be coldblooded killers, not me. I said I'd stay and I will."

Carl glanced at Nick. Nick shrugged. "You heard the lady."

He sighed hard. "I'll go. But I damn well don't like it."

"Duly noted, Salducci. Now get the hell outta here."

She didn't miss the affection in Nick's eyes, and once again her certainty that he was no criminal outweighed her doubt. In fact, she didn't believe either one of them was working for Taranto. She'd never come across a gentler man than Carl.

He left, albeit reluctantly. Toni scrutinized Nick's face from her perch on the edge of the bed. "He cares a lot for just an acquaintance."

"Don't miss a trick, do you?"

She sighed at the tautness in his voice. "It's odd, but I'm not entirely comfortable with the door unlocked. I can't tell the good guys from the bad guys."

"You don't want to tell," he replied.

"You're wrong about that."

He dropped his gaze. "If you hear anyone coming, pull the door open and close it again. The lock will take automatically." He closed his eyes, then forced them open. "If you leave tonight, Toni, take my gun with you. Get on the first flight out of the country and—"

"I am not going anywhere. What is it with you? Don't you trust *anyone?*" His lips tightened into a thin line. "You don't, do you?"

"No. I don't."

She looked at the floor, then at his face again. "Is that why you won't tell me the truth?"

"Are you still fantasizing? Look, I need to get some sleep. I can barely keep my eyes open."

It was frustrating the way he kept her guessing. Still, he had admitted to a weakness rather than discuss whether he was or was not being honest with her. Maybe that should tell her something. "So sleep then."

She leaned closer to him and unbuckled the strap that held his shoulder holster around his body. He stiffened, and his eyes flew open again. "Easy, big guy. I'm only trying to make you comfortable. You can't go to sleep as you are."

He relaxed and let her take the holster from him, gun and all. She put it aside, then began unbuttoning his shirt. "Just how 'comfortable' are you planning on making me?"

"Still have a sense of humor, I see." She helped

him sit up a little and tried to ignore the feel of his firm biceps as she pushed the material down them and eased his arms from the sleeves. She refused to look at his chest. She wasn't lying to herself anymore. There was a strong physical attraction here. But just because she admitted it to herself didn't mean she had to give in to it.

She eased him back onto the pillows, and then tore the outside seams of his trousers so she could remove them. They were ruined anyway. He watched her without comment. "Brace with your good leg," she told him. "Lift your hips just a little." When he complied, she slid the pants from beneath him. He wore white boxers underneath. She kept her eyes averted and grabbed up the clean cloth from the basin of soapy water. Deftly she washed the remaining blood from the length of his leg and patted it dry with a clean towel. She took the whiskey-and-blood-dampened towel from beneath his leg and swiped the wet cloth over the back of his thigh. "Almost done," she told him, taking the basin to dump it again. "Then I'll let you sleep."

When she returned, it was with another clean washcloth.

This time she wiped a streak of blood from his face. She put the cloth in his hand. "Here. You can do your own hands." He did. Toni gave one last, worried glance at the patch of white on his thigh and pulled the covers over him.

"You gonna read me a bedtime story, too?" His voice was heavy with sarcasm but heavier with exhaustion.

"I'm not going to fight with you tonight, so you can quit trying." She tucked the blankets around him. "Now, is there anything else you need before you go to sleep? Another shot of whiskey? Some more Ibuprofen?"

"No. I'm fine."

"Okay, then." She gathered up the bandages, the discarded wrappers, the ruined pants and dropped all of it into a plastic bag. Then she looked down at her yoga pants, which she'd put on for easy running, and saw they were smeared with his blood. Her hands were, as well. A shower was definitely in order. "I just need to clean up, but I'll turn off the light so you can rest. I don't want you to move, Nick." She chewed her lip, hating to leave him alone in case the bleeding should start up again. "I'll leave the door open. Yell if—"

"It's my thigh, not a damn kidney. I've hurt myself worse than this playing basketball."

She ignored him and went into the bathroom for a record-fast shower. She pulled on an oversized hockey jersey, her favorite sleepwear, and tiptoed back into the bedroom. Pulling a chair nearer the bed as quietly as she could, she sat down in it.

"What are you doing?" His head turn in her direction as he spoke.

"I'm sitting. What does it look like I'm doing?"

"You don't have to sit there all night. I'm okay. Go sack out on the couch."

"No thanks. Wouldn't sleep a wink out there,

anyway."

"Why, for crying out loud?"

"Because you might need me. Whether you'll admit it or not, Nick, that's more than a scratch. You lost a lot of blood and you are not out of the woods yet. If you need me, I want to be close."

He blew a short sigh. "I won't. I don't need anyone. I never freaking have."

"Well, I'll be here, just the same, in case you ever freaking do."

CHAPTER 7

Nick lay awake for a long time, despite his feeling of having been wrung out like a wet rag. He watched Toni, certain she'd get up and walk out before long. She wouldn't get far if she did. The door was unlocked, yes, but if he thought she had a chance in hell of making it off the grounds without his knowledge, he wouldn't have had Carl leave it that way. If she got away, she'd end up dead. He wasn't sure why he'd blurted the warning he had, about taking his gun and leaving the country. He supposed it was because he'd lost so much blood and wasn't thinking too clearly. Or maybe because he had to admit there was a slim chance she could escape. She was resourceful. And gutsy.

He never for a minute thought he'd take a turn for the worse and need help. Leaving the door unlocked was completely unnecessary, the way he saw it. Part of him, though, needed to see her leave. He wasn't even sure why, but he needed to see her do it. He needed to be reminded, in no uncertain terms, that people couldn't be trusted. They left you the minute your defenses were down.

She didn't leave, though. He watched her small form silhouetted in the half light for as long as he could stay awake, and she never left. After a while her head fell to one side. Her breathing grew deeper and took on the rhythm of sleep. He couldn't believe it, wouldn't have, if the proof hadn't been right there in front of him. When he fell asleep, it was in a state of confusion. She hadn't left. But she still might. Maybe she hadn't got from him all that she wanted just yet. Maybe she'd wait until morning.

For a time his mind relaxed in blissful darkness, but then something changed. The lights came up slowly, and the stage was set. Danny lay on the rotted wood floor, pale and blue lipped. Nick shook him, but he barely had strength enough to do so. He felt incredibly weak and clumsy and colder than he could remember being in his life. Still, he recited the lines he knew by heart. "Don't die on me. Hold on, Danny, hold on. Don't die...don't leave me, damn you."

The young Nick in the dream thought he must have caught his leg on a nail on the way into this dump. His thigh was screaming. It felt hot and it throbbed like a toothache. He didn't care—he didn't care if the damn thing fell off, not when Danny's life hung in the balance. "You're all I got, man. Don't do this—Danny? Danny!"

The scene faded, but he knew it was there, just

out of sight. Something cold and wet lay across his forehead. Another cold thing pressed to that spot on his thigh. God, it felt good. His head was pulled upward, small things between his lips...pills, then the lip of a glass and icy cold water.

"Drink, Nick. Swallow. You have a fever."

He followed the instructions of that musical voice. The glass moved away, and he muttered something. He wasn't sure what. But it came back. He drank and drank. He couldn't remember being this thirsty. When the water was gone, his body moved until his head was cradled in a pillow of warm flesh, familiar scent. He knew that scent. "Toni," he muttered.

"I'm right here." Cool hands stroked his cheeks and his hair in soothing, slow movements. The cloth left his forehead, and he heard water trickling. It came back colder.

"You...didn't leave?"

"I told you I wouldn't."

He hovered between the reality of the woman who held him and the memory of the dream. "Danny—"

"I know." Her cool hands stilled on his face. "It was a long time ago, Nick. Danny is gone. He's at peace. I'm here with you now, though, and I won't leave."

"You will." Nick let his mind drift back into the comforting blackness. The pain from his thigh had lessened. It no longer burned. "They all do."

Nick woke with his head in Toni's lap. Her palm rested motionless on his cheek, and he realized with a start that she'd been in that same position for several hours, stroking his head and his face as he drifted in and out of sleep. A glance at the clock's luminous dial told him there was still over an hour before dawn.

She sat with her back against the headboard, her legs curled beneath her. Nick's head lay on her uppermost thigh. Her chin touched her chest, and a frown had etched itself between her brows, even in sleep. Without moving, Nick shifted his gaze. On the nightstand a basin of water sat beside an opened bottle of pain reliever, an empty glass and two soaking-wet cloths. He tried to remember what had happened during the night to get Toni from her chair beside the bed to where she now slept. Only fragments came to him. He remembered pain and pills being pushed between his lips and the welcome coldness of the water. He remembered her voice— her touch.

My God, she's still here.

He studied her face as she slept and realized fully what she'd done. She'd held him all night and she'd done her damnedest to keep the pain at bay. She'd spoken softly to him, words of comfort. His own mother had never treated him with the tenderness Toni had. And she'd promised not to leave.

He was still staring at her face when her heavy lashes lifted, revealing to him yet again those glistening, fathomless dark eyes. He saw them narrow at once, felt the hand on his face tense and move to his forehead as it had done many times during the night. Finding no more than a normal amount of heat emanating from his skin, she smiled.

"How do you feel now?"

He shrugged. "All right, I guess." The silken warmth of her bare thigh under his cheek was distracting. He lifted his head so she could slip out from under him. She moved slightly to the side, stretched her legs out fully beside him, hooked one hand at the back of her neck and rubbed. "What happened last night?" he asked.

"Your temperature spiked. I'm afraid you have a nasty infection trying to set in." She met his gaze. "You don't remember?"

"Bits and pieces."

She nodded thoughtfully. "I'm not surprised. You were quite...disoriented." She swung her feet to the floor. "I ought to change that bandage, see how bad it is."

"Not yet." Nick sat up, and she turned to face him. "What do you mean by 'disoriented'?" He hadn't liked the emphasis she put on the word.

She tilted her head to one side. "You did a lot of talking. Do you want some of that whiskey before I unwrap—"

"What did I say?"

She looked away from his eyes. "You told me everything. I know you're a cop. Don't worry, your secret is safe. I just don't know why you didn't tell me in the first place. This whole ordeal would've been so much easier if you'd just..."

Nick felt the blood drain from his face as she rambled on. He couldn't believe he'd been that feverish...that he'd blurt something like that and not even remember. He caught himself then, watched her as she spoke. She was talking too fast and she never met his gaze.

"What kind of cop?"

She broke off at his interruption, looked at him slowly, her face blank. "Well— I—um—I guess you didn't say."

He smiled and shook his head in silent admiration of her brass. "Nice try, Toni. I didn't say anything like that. I know, because it's bull. A figment of your creative imagination."

To his surprise she smiled, too, like a cat leaving a pet store with feathers in its whiskers. "I don't think so. You believed me for just a second. You wouldn't have if there wasn't some slight chance you might've said what I just told you you did." The smile died slowly. She held his gaze, her own eyes going softer. "It was a mean trick to play on a guy as sick as you were last night. I'm sorry. It was either that or go on questioning my sanity—not a healthy alternative."

"Your sanity isn't an issue here. It left the day you started with this imaginary secret identity of mine."

She shrugged, stood up and carefully peeled away the tape that held the bandages. "You are one stubborn SOB, Nick Manelli."

He didn't answer her. He couldn't just then. The concern that clouded her face as she unwound the bandage and gently peeled away the gauze pads was too convincing. Maybe even real. She cleaned the wound once more, applied an abundance of ointment and re-wrapped it, taking great care not to hurt him. "Tell you what," she said as she worked. "Since you're in a weakened state, I'll drop this subject—for now—if you'll do something for me."

"To drop this, lady, you could damn near name your price."

Her dark brows shot up. "Well, now, that will require some thought. Normally, when I'm told I can have anything I want, I demand chocolate, but—"

"Chocolate? Chocolate what?"

"Oh, anything. I'm a confirmed chocoholic." She taped the gauze down and looked at him seriously. "But in this case, I'd prefer conversation." Nick's wariness returned in force, but she hurried on. "Not about what you're not telling me or what I'm not telling you. I want you to tell me about *you*. The way I told you about me last night. About my dad, and—"

"What do you want to know?" He still wasn't sure this was anything but another attempt to get the truth from him.

She turned from his thigh, pulling herself fully onto the bed and facing him. "You did talk last night, when the fever shot up. You talked about Danny." Nick felt the old pain twist within him but concealed it. "Your brother, right?"

Nick nodded. "My brother's death is not my favorite topic of conversation."

"Of course it isn't. I heard enough about that last

night." Compassion made her voice thick. "It must have been awful for you." He said nothing. "But what was it like before all that?" He frowned at her. "I never had an older brother—not that I know of anyway—but I always wanted one."

What was she doing? Why did she want to stir up his most painful memory? Didn't she realize that he couldn't think of Danny without thinking of that horrible night in the condemned building? He hadn't—not from that day to this. His only memory of his brother was of those last few minutes in the filthy building with the sirens and flashing lights outside. Of his pasty skin and lifeless eyes. It wasn't possible to remember anything else.

"I always wanted siblings. Had an imaginary sister when I was very small, you know. She walked me to school that first day. When I was afraid of the dark, she was always in my bedroom with me. Sometimes we'd talk all night long—or it seemed that way."

"Danny was the one who brought home all the jigsaw puzzles." Nick hadn't intended to say the words. They slipped out, from some unseen crack into his subconscious. "There was never a lot of money—puzzles were cheap. Some nights we'd sit up until two in the morning trying to finish a new one." He felt something tugging the corners of his lips upward, suddenly recalling the two of them sitting on the bedroom floor trying to do a puzzle by flashlight and fighting off attacks of laughter that were sure to wake their mother.

"He was a year older, but way smaller," he went

on. "He had the greenest eyes, and Fiona's red hair. If you'd seen the two of us together, you wouldn't believe we were related."

He shook his head slowly, in awe. But Toni didn't give him time to think about what had just happened to him. "That's like my sister Joey and me. We look so different."

"No, not around the eyes," he said, looking at her pretty eyes, getting kind of lost in the light that was waiting there.

"I got one of those circular jigsaws for my birthday one year," she said. "Remember those? They were really tough."

Nick's mind returned him to that bedroom floor, with a circular jigsaw in front of him depicting Superman in flight, an adoring Lois Lane in his arms. And Danny, wondering aloud why one of Superman's hands wasn't visible in the picture and whether or not it was inside Lois's skirt. They'd laughed so loudly over that one, they were sure they'd be caught. And every time one of them managed to stop laughing, the other one would start again and in seconds they'd both be rolling on the floor, red faced and breathless.

He didn't even realize he was telling her about it as he remembered, and a minute later Toni was laughing. *Nick was laughing.* He was *laughing.* And when he stopped, he looked at her and shook his head. "How did you do that?"

She smiled at him and parted her lips to speak, then stopped. The smile died and her gaze focused beyond him, through the doorway into the living room. "Nick, the light—the little red light on the panel—"

He looked that way too. "Someone's at the front gate." He glanced again at the clock and could think of only one person who'd show up at this hour. "You'd better grab me some clothes."

She nodded and hurried to the closet, taking down a starched white shirt and a pair of the trousers.

Nick swung his legs over the side of the bed and felt the instant return of the pain in his thigh. Toni knelt and slipped the pants over his feet and up his legs. She made him lean on her when he stood to pull them up. She held the shirt for him to slip his arms into its sleeves.

He thought of the monitor as he buttoned the shirt, but before he'd decided whether it would be safe to share that secret with her, she was running into the living room, moving a kitchen chair to the bookshelf, and climbing up onto it to grab the remote. She pointed it at the big screen and turned it on. Nick limped into the room to glance at the screen and then, incredulously, at Toni. "When did you—"

"Within the first twenty-four hours. It's Taranto, isn't it?"

Nick looked at the gray Mercedes at the gate, its wipers beating uselessly against the slashing rain, its headlights pale in the storm's darkness. He nodded. He wanted nothing more right now than to sit Toni down and make her tell him how she knew about high-tech surveillance devices, but he had to deal with Lou first. "I'll have to go down and talk to him." He took the remote from her.

He started for the door, but her hand gripped his shoulder with surprising force. "You can't go down all those stairs on that leg."

"It's either that or invite him up here." He saw the worry in her dark eyes and knew it was genuine and for him. He reached down and touched her face, trailing the backs of his fingers from her delicate, high cheekbone to her impertinent chin. She'd given him a precious thing in the hours before this dawn: the knowledge that he could remember Danny as he'd been before—when they'd been brothers in every sense of the word. When they'd been happy. How could he tell her what that meant?

His fingertips in the hollow under her chin, he tilted her head up and lowered his own. His lips brushed over hers. She didn't pull away. He kissed her again, pressing his lips fully to hers, parting them with the tip of his tongue. He still held only his fingertips to her chin. He wanted to sweep her into his arms—to pick up where they'd left off last night before he'd said the things he had.

She stepped away, avoiding his eyes. "Taranto," she reminded him.

He nodded and went to the door. She didn't even try to see the numbers he punched, but when he pulled the door open, she was at his side again, her hand on the knob. "Be careful on the stairs," she warned. "Don't put too much weight on the leg."

He closed the door with her still muttering that

he at least ought to have a cane of some sort. And she was right. The stairs were torture, but he made his way down both flights and let Lou Taranto in the front door a few seconds later.

Lou burst in, hugged Nick like a long-lost son and urged him down onto the leather sofa. He moved behind the bar as if he owned it, poured two shots and waved a fleshy hand toward the mousy man who scurried in his wake. "My personal physician, Nicky. Also my nephew. I put him through med school. He returns the favor when I need him." He slammed a shot glass into Nick's hand. "Jake and Sly, filled me in. Down it, Nicky. Then drop the pants. David! Get over here and take a look."

Nick glanced at the guy who jumped when Lou bellowed his name. He was pale, thin, and the round wire rims perched on his nose made him look ten years older than he probably was. His hair was rumpled, as if he'd been yanked out of bed for the occasion. He stepped up to Nick, black bag in hand. Nick swallowed the whiskey, stood up and dropped his pants. You didn't argue when Lou Taranto offered to do you a favor. He sat down again, ignoring the small man who began to unwrap the wound.

"The boys say you saved their asses last night."

Nick affected a derisive snort. "A lot of good it did. We lost the shipment. And Rosco."

Lou swallowed half his whiskey and shrugged. "Too bad about Rosco. But I prefer dead to jailed. He went out with honor—not like Vinnie, eh?" He laughed, a low rumble that seemed to gain momentum as it moved through him. "As for the shipment, what the hell? Easy come, easy go, right, Nicky?"

Nick frowned, an uneasy suspicion settling in the pit of his stomach. "You don't care about the shipment?"

"It's gone. Whining about it won't bring it back. I can afford the loss."

Nick studied his face and realized Fat Lou couldn't care less about the heroin that had been confiscated. "How much did we lose?"

Lou pursed his lips. "What difference does it make?"

He was wondering about all Nick's questions. Nick shrugged quickly. "Not a damn bit to me. How many cops did we take out, anyway?"

Lou drained his glass and slammed it on the polished surface. "Not a damn one."

"Good."

Lou's head snapped around. Even David stopped what he was doing and looked up quickly. "What the hell do you mean, 'good'?"

"Think about it, Lou. This way the cops think they've won one. They grabbed a major haul without losing a single man—didn't they?" Lou frowned and didn't answer, so Nick rushed on. "They took out one of Lou Taranto's men to boot. They'll be so busy patting themselves on the back, making speeches and taking interviews, they won't have time to bother us for a while. On the other hand, if we'd shot a cop or two—"

"They'd be out for blood," Lou finished. "You're a sharp one, Nicky. I'm glad you're not working for the enemy."

For once Nick's smile wasn't forced. David was already rewrapping the leg and not doing half the job Toni had, Nick thought. He was glad when the man finished and rose.

"I don't know who tended this for you," he commented, "but they did a nice job. Slight infection trying to take hold. I'll leave something for it." He rummaged in his bag as Nick stood and righted his trousers.

"Who fixed you up last night, Nicky? You holdin' out on me? Got a woman stashed around here?"

The question startled him. He hadn't anticipated it and he should have. Any hesitation would arouse Lou's suspicion, and his answer might well be checked out. "The new guy—what's his name?"

"Carl?" Lou's brows lifted, two silvery arches above a bulbous, slightly red nose.

"That's it. Hell of a man," Nick told him. "Drove like a pro, dropped the kids where it was safe, lost the cops. Then he stuck around long enough to patch me up. I would've bled to death if he hadn't."

Lou puckered in thought. "I'll see he gets a bonus, then." He looked down at David, who was bent nearly double, squinting at the label of a small brown bottle. "You about done?"

David jumped as if someone had pinched him. "Uh, yes. Here." He set the bottle on the coffee table. It tipped over. "Antibiotics. Directions are on the label." He pulled a tube of ointment from his bag, set it beside the toppled plastic bottle, snapped the bag shut and hurried to the door. He couldn't seem to get out of there fast enough.

Nick glanced at Lou. "You scared him."

Lou shook his head. "So does his shadow. I wanted to talk to you alone."

"About?"

"The girl. I know who she was."

"The girl?" Nick feigned ignorance.

"The one that you popped. She's trouble."

"You still on that, Lou? She's dead. How's she trouble?"

"You're sure?"

Nick released a deliberate bark of laughter. "Damn, don't you think I can tell a dead woman from a live one?"

Lou smiled at that. "Sure I do, Nicky. I just wish you'd have asked her name first."

"Like I told you before, she saw the hit, she had to go. Who she was was irrelevant."

"Yeah, well, maybe not so irrelevant as we thought. Viper thought he'd seen her somewhere before. When they flashed her picture on the local news, he realized where. She'd been hanging around the club the past few weeks." Lou blew air through puckered lips and shook his head. "Big headline, you know. Missing, Antonia del Rio. Only they aren't saying who she really is. Not yet anyway. I wondered—checked with my informant inside NYPD."

Nick shook his head, not following at all. What

would Toni have been doing at the Century?

Lou reached inside his voluminous coat and pulled out a hardcover book. On the front of the glossy black jacket was a lamppost with a shadowy figure leaning against it, feminine calves outlined beneath a trench coat, ending in stiletto heels. Huge red letters marched across the top: Poison Profits. Across the bottom was written in equally large letters, Toni Rio.

The truth slammed into Nick like a freight train. He came to his feet so fast it jarred his thigh. "You've got to be kidding me."

Lou tossed the book down as if it were dirty. "No joke. Bitch wrote this last year. Raised so much hell I lost my blow supplier. Took me six months to set up a new partnership. She knew stuff about the business I didn't even know. She was good."

Nick didn't need Lou to tell him about the elusive Toni Rio. The bureau had a file on the woman that read like *War and Peace*. Her works were fiction, but the stuff she used to sweeten those plots was real and the whole world knew it. The lady sleuth she'd created—Katrina Chekov—waltzed from one taboo subject to another, shattering myths along the way and always putting the bad guys on ice.

That was no more than every Fed knew. If he'd actually read that file of hers, he might have known before now that her full name was Antonia Veronica Rosa del Rio—and that she looked like a small Mayan princess. Rumor had it she was working on a new fictionalized exposé, one that would blow the lid off the Taranto crime family. Lou had to know that.

Nick cleared his throat. "Dead is dead, Lou. Even if she was some kind of celeb—"

"Don't you follow, Nicky? She was writing a book about me! She wasn't in that alley by accident. And if she knew enough to be there, she knew way too much. Who the hell knows what she has down on paper, just waiting for some nosy damn Fed to find—"

"It's fiction, for God's sake!"

"The book, maybe. But what about the notes—the research, or whatever the hell she'd call it? Man, to know about the hit, she had to be into us deep." Lou shook his head. "I'm sending some guys to her place tonight—tellin' 'em to tear it apart. And if they don't find everything she had on us there, I'll have 'em lean on her family. She must'a had a family. In fact, I got a line on a half sister up Syracuse way."

"Wait just a damn minute," Nick barked. There was no more time to feel his way. He had to take the offensive here and now or lose the chance. "This was my mess. I should've wrung the truth out of her before I took her out. For once in his worthless life, Viper was right. *I* loused this up. *I* oughtta fix it."

"Like how?" Lou was listening. Nick knew he'd better make it good, or the game was over.

"I can get in and out of her place without anyone knowing I was there. If there's anything to find, I'll find it. Hell, I'll bring it to you. I'll personally light the match for you, and we'll watch it burn over drinks at the commission meeting. Be the highlight of the night."

Lou nodded once, then pinned Nick to the spot with an intense glint in his eyes. "And if you don't find anything? You got the stomach to rough up the sister?"

Nick smiled slowly. "I got ways of getting information that Viper doesn't even have nightmares about. Let me handle it, Lou. I'll let you watch when things get nasty."

Lou's grin split his face. Nick knew the man's perverse appetite for watching people suffer. He was a sadist once removed—too soft to inflict the pain himself.

"All right, Nicky. All right. But I gotta have results by the meeting. I can't let it go beyond that. The other bosses are nervous as hell. If you can't get what I need, I'll send in someone who can."

Nick nodded. "I'll get it, Lou. It'll be the finishing touch for my initiation, don't you think?"

When Nick had left the room, taking the remote with him, Toni had followed, shouting warnings as a distraction and holding the doorknob in her hand as he pulled it shut. She hadn't let it close all the way, so the lock did not engage. As soon as Nick's footsteps had faded, she opened the bookcase door and silently followed. She would not sit still while he went down there, wounded and alone, to face Lou Taranto and whoever was with him. She didn't like the odds. Besides, she had to hear this conversation. She'd convinced herself again that Nick couldn't possibly be in Taranto's employ. The man he was when he was alone with her was not that kind. Granted, he was entirely different when he was with Taranto. She had to know, once and for all, which Nick was the real one.

She sat just out of sight and well within earshot at the top of the curving stairway. All the air left her lungs in a rush when she heard Nick make the offer he just had. Her throat tightened until she couldn't swallow, and her eyes were scalding. He'd sounded ruthless, vicious.

Not the Nick I know, she told herself as she struggled to contain the panic she felt spreading like ice water through her veins. *He wouldn't hurt my sister—he promised. This is just an act.*

Maybe, she thought. And maybe not. She wanted to trust Nick. More than anything, she wanted to believe her instinct that he wasn't capable of such cruelty, that he truly was the gentle, caring man she'd come to know. She felt it so strongly she would have trusted him with her life.

But can I trust him with my sister's? And if there's even a one-in-a-million chance I'm wrong....

She shook herself. She couldn't think objectively about Nick. Her attraction to him always got in the way. And her sister was obviously in jeopardy now, if not from Nick then from Taranto himself. She had to get out of there, get to Joey, warn her.

Nearly frantic as she fought with images of what the filthy Viper might do to her sister, Toni jumped when Nick stood to walk Lou to the front door. Then she saw her opportunity. She raced down both flights of stairs as soon as they were out of sight and ducked into a small room off the opposite end of the living room. She had only one thought in mind. She had to protect her sister. She'd failed her father; let him leave when her instincts had told her to stop him. She wouldn't repeat the mistake.

She held her breath and waited, giving Taranto ample time to drive away and Nick time to remount the stairs and, she hoped, reach the third floor. It would take him longer than usual, due to the bullet wound. She tried to be patient, knowing he'd try to stop her, no matter which side he was truly on. She couldn't let that happen.

When she thought enough time had passed, she moved to the nearest window. It faced the rear of the house, and beyond it she could see only darkness and slashing rain. It was locked, naturally. She was out of patience with Nick and his locks. She picked up the first thing she saw, a marble sculpture of a rearing stallion, and hurled it right through the glass. If only Nick had been honest with her, none of this would be necessary. A tiny voice of doubt whispered in the back of her mind that it might be more necessary than ever, but she refused to listen.

She climbed through the window, her only thought that she had to save her sister. She had no plan of action, no thought of getting past the gate or of how to reach Joey in time to protect her. With her knack for knowing things before they happened, maybe

Joey would know, and take precautions, but Toni couldn't depend on that. She had no qualms about running into the fury of a summer storm dressed in nothing but an oversize shirt and her underwear. She didn't feel the jagged shard that raked across her upper arm. She didn't flinch from the bits of glass that jabbed into the bottoms of her bare feet as she made her way over the wet ground and away from the hulking gray stone mansion.

CHAPTER 8

When Nick walked through the third-floor study and found the bookcase standing slightly away from the wall, all the blood rushed to his feet. He moved quickly into the apartment, knowing already that he wouldn't find her there. He felt the emptiness in every room as if it were a presence in itself. He didn't need the flashing light to confirm it. He shut off the system before the alarm bell could start in.

Where the hell was she? Somewhere on the grounds, he rationalized. She had to be—she wouldn't take off. Not now. Unless... Nick's gaze moved to the monitor. Unless she'd overheard his conversation with Lou and believed his act. But she couldn't have. He had taken the remote...

...and dropped it on the table in the study as he rushed through. He turned now and went to find it still resting there, beside the unplugged telephone. He grabbed both items and ducked back into the apartment. He

inserted the phone's cord into its jack, punched in Carl's number with one hand, thumbed the monitor to life with the other. He was scanning each room for a sign of Toni when Carl picked up.

"I'm calling it," he said without prelude. "Pull out, Carl."

"What do you mean, 'pull out'? Are you nuts? We just—"

Nick continued flicking buttons on the remote, his gaze intent on the screen. "Lou's too damn unconcerned about losing that shipment. Almost like he expected it. It stinks of a setup, Carl. He staged it. A loyalty test. And I don't know which of us he was testing. But he's gotta know one of the men who was at that warehouse last night tipped off the cops. Pull out now, and watch your back."

Carl swore. "Okay. All right, if you say so. Listen, how's the leg? I—"

"Later. I have to move." Nick replaced the receiver slowly. He'd stopped flicking buttons when he'd seen the small sitting room with the smashed window. "My God, if she was in there..."

He closed his eyes slowly, opened them again. She had heard everything. And she'd obviously believed every word he'd said to Lou. He shook himself and went into the bedroom, yanked a dresser drawer completely out and flipped it upside down on the bed. Now that it didn't matter, she believed his cover story. Her timing was damn near awful. He tore free the envelope taped to the bottom of the drawer, ripped it open and took from it a small leather folder the size of a wallet. Slipping it into his pocket, he ran unevenly back through the apartment and down the stairs, ignoring the stabbing pain each step sent shooting through his leg.

In the little sitting room at the bottom of the stairs, the wind blew the curtains wildly. Rain slanted in, wetting the floor and the wall beneath the window. Nick paused only long enough to find a flashlight and then he climbed out the same way Toni had, noting the trace of blood on a pointed finger of glass. On the ground, he squinted through the downpour to try to make out her shape in the darkness. He aimed the flashlight's beam onto the muddied ground in search of her small footprints. If anything happened to her, he would never forgive himself.

Toni slipped in the rain-slick grass more than once as she ran from the mansion. She decided not to go near the front gate, certain that would be the first place Nick would look for her, and instead, headed for the woods behind the house. Maybe the place wasn't as secure as he'd said. There might not be fencing all the way around, and even if there was, there might be some way over or under or through it.

The trees closed themselves behind her as soon as she breached the first cluster of them, hiding the house from her view. She stumbled onward, rain streaming between her shoulder blades. It had plastered the hockey jersey she wore to her skin and soaked her hair within minutes. Her limp curls stuck to her face and neck, heavy and wet and cold. She had to blink raindrops from her eyes every few steps just to see where she was going, but she pushed on, trying to keep to a straight course, refusing to think or to feel. Her every sense was focused on moving, on seeing through the rain and on putting as much distance between herself and Nick Manelli as she could.

She resisted the subconscious masochist that wanted to replay, over and over in her mind, the horrible things she'd heard Nick say. She didn't want to hear again the change in his voice from the moment Taranto had told him who she really was. She didn't want to wonder if that knowledge had made a difference to him...had made him hate her as much as it sounded like he did.

A sob tore at her throat as those thoughts ran through her mind, despite her determination not to let them. The seed of doubt grew larger. As the trees grew closer together, they blunted the force of the rain. Pines, she realized dully as their needles continued brushing her arms and their scent reached out to offer solace. The wind couldn't slash at her there. The rain still came through, but more gently, filtered through the boughs. The ground seemed to sink under her feet, as if she was walking on soft sponges instead of several inches of wet, browning needles. They made a carpet for her cold, bare feet.

She slowed her pace, beginning to feel the biting shards of glass she'd stepped on, and the painful cut in her right shoulder. Eventually she had to stop. She'd walked for what seemed a very long distance and still hadn't come to a fence demarcating the border of the property. Bracing one hand against the sticky trunk of a pine, she heard its needles whispering above her head as the rain hissed down through them to sprinkle her. She glanced around but could see no farther than two or three trees in any direction. The glimpses of sky she could catch between the sheltering arms of the pines showed her only a bleak, gray thing—the perfect sky to match the way she felt. She couldn't understand the intense pain that seemed lodged in the center of her chest. But she knew it grew with every step she took...and each time she felt herself doubting Nick, it grew even more.

She bit her lower lip, and a chill rushed through her as the wind found its way to her bare legs. Had she allowed herself to indulge in a silly infatuation? Had she deluded herself with a fantasy image of a man who didn't exist?

She thought about last night when her heart had iced over at the sight of his blood-soaked leg. All she'd wanted was to ease his pain, to make him all right. She'd held him when his fever had climbed. She'd rocked him in her arms as she would her own child, and she'd felt the wrenching pain in him when he'd dreamed of his brother. Toni had convinced herself that no man who'd loved a brother as he had could work for Lou Taranto.

It couldn't have all been in her imagination. Even

now, she wished she could turn around and run back to him, fall into those big, strong arms and pour out her fears as he held her and promised her that everything would be all right. Only fear for her sister kept her from doing just that...fear and a kernel of doubt that wouldn't let go.

She folded her arms against the tree and lowered her head to them. "God," she moaned softly. "How could I have been so wrong about him all along?"

"You weren't wrong, Toni."

His voice was so near her ear that she stiffened in shock, then pivoted, flattening her back to the wet, stringy bark to see him standing mere inches from her. "Don't try to take me back, Nick. I have to go to her...I have to—"

He caught her hand in one of his, turned it slowly and pressed the flashlight he held into it. He folded her fingers around it as Toni frowned and shook her head, not understanding. She opened her mouth to ask what he wanted from her, but his finger pressed to her lips and silenced her. He caught her other hand and lifted it, palm up. He took something from his pocket and lay it flat on her palm.

Her fingers closed over the leather, brought it to her face for a better look and caught the scent of it. It was folded in half. She looked at Nick, and a crazy hope leapt up in her breast as she opened the folder and lifted the light to it. The shield glowed in the white light, right beside the photo ID. Nick's face, unsmiling, beside his full name, Nicholas Anthony Manelli, and the words Federal Bureau of

Investigation.

Every muscle went limp and Toni swore her bones melted. Her hands fell to her sides, and her eyes closed. Nick took the folder from her unresisting fingers and then the light. His hands came back to her, huge and strong, closing on her shoulders, pulling her away from the solid tree. She gladly traded its support for that of his equally solid chest as his arms closed around her. Feeling as if she'd been standing alone in a hurricane, she encircled his neck with her arms, pressed her head to his chest so that it rose and fell with every breath he took. Her goose-bump-covered legs were flush with his, separated only by a thin barrier of wet cloth.

When his arms loosened from her waist, she knew he would lead her back to the house. She didn't want to go. She didn't feel strong enough to stand if he stopped holding her, and clung shamelessly. His head tipped backward, as if he were seeking help from above. A moment later his big hand cupped her head, cradling it more securely to his chest. His other arm closed once more around her waist, providing her with the support she'd sought, holding her tight against him. His head came down, and she felt his lips in her hair, at the very top of her head.

Toni looked up into his eyes, and found them even darker than the stormy predawn sky. The emotion in them reached her and found its mate within her. She felt her response begin deep in the pit of her stomach before his lips claimed hers. And when they did, it became a fire that tried to consume them both.

Clutching at his shoulder with one hand, she buried the other in his hair and pulled him closer. She kissed him hungrily, unable to get enough of him. He groaned as his hands slid down over her hips and beyond the edge of the shirt to her rain-slick thighs. And when she arched against him and he shuddered in response, she wondered at her ability to inspire such a reaction in him—a man so beautiful it hurt to look at him.

She worked one of her hands between them and flicked open the buttons of his shirt. When she gained access, she ran her hand over his chest, dragging her nails lightly over his skin and hearing his ragged breath. Impatient now that she was sure of herself, she pushed his shirt down over his shoulders and seared his chest with her kisses and her rapid, shallow breaths. She felt the cool rain on her flushed skin, her upturned face, and the chill breeze that played across her thighs. She felt everything.

Nick lowered her down with him, onto the cool wet blanket of needles until they knelt there together. He peeled her jersey off over her head, and spread it on the ground behind her.

When his eyes met hers, she felt no shyness. His hungry gaze moved over her, leaving no part of her untouched. She felt feminine in every cell of her body because of that gaze. She felt more attractive, more female, more powerful than she had in her life. And when he lay down, pulling her on top of him, wrapping himself around her, rocking her slowly, she felt as if she'd come home. They made love there in the pouring rain, tenderly and slowly, exploring and learning each other, whispering and caressing. Their mouths barely parted, and the passion grew. He was so careful with her, and until she didn't want him to be. And then he took her to the stars.

Toni lay there, relaxed on top of him, cradled is his arms that were so big they protected her from the rain. She heard his heard pounding, felt the heat of his skin, and closed her eyes. It was perfection. It was bliss. And she would never forget this time, or this man, no matter what might lie ahead for them.

His mind kept telling him it was not possible. His body disagreed. It made no sense. It couldn't have been as explosive as it had seemed. Nothing could be. It had felt like being caught in a hurricane and carried through its violence to the paradise at its eye.

Now he had the craziest urge to rock her small body against his—to kiss every inch of her until she either fell asleep in his arms or asked for more—to brush some of that wet, wavy hair away from her face and look into her eyes and tell her—

"What am I, insane?"

He rolled away from her as the words burst from him without permission. He sat up and held his head in his hands.

She sat up beside him, her shoulder pressed to his. "You think it was insane to make love to me?"

Make love. God, he wished she wouldn't call it that.

It hadn't been that. He wasn't stupid enough to have let it be that. He said the first thing that came to mind, realizing she expected some kind of answer. "Out here, like this, yeah. Insane. You'll probably have pneumonia."

He turned toward her to see what she thought of that answer. She was sitting with her knees slightly bent, toes playing in the pine needles. Her breasts were already dotted with raindrops again. Nick closed his eyes. "Put your shirt on, Toni, you've got to be chilled through."

Frowning a little, she stood, shook out the shirt and pulled it on. When she reached for her panties, he turned his back and busied himself replacing his own clothes. They were wet, which made it difficult, but he wasn't about to march back to the house stark naked. The way he felt every time he looked at her, he'd never make it. When he turned again, she was watching him, a puzzled expression on her face.

"Is something wrong?"

Good question, Nick thought. No, nothing's wrong; everything's just the way it should be. Good ol' gullible Nick has let himself care again, and sure as the sun will rise tomorrow, he's going to get left high and dry again. Toni would walk away from him. One way or another, she'd leave him. He had no one to blame but himself, because he'd known it would happen. He'd told himself not to feel anything for her. The problem was, his self hadn't listened. The only thing left to do now was to prepare for the blow. He had a feeling it was going to be a tough one to take. Maybe too tough. Maybe this would be the one that brought him down.

"Nick?"

Her hand on his face sent a shaft of bleak pain through him. He nearly winced at the strength of it. The most he could hope for now, he realized, was a little damage control. He could only avoid total devastation by keeping his feelings for her from growing any stronger. He'd always been a man of action—never content to let anything slip beyond his ability to control it. He could do this, he told himself. He could keep this thing on a purely physical level. He could force his feelings for her to die quietly, before she had the chance to throw them back in his face. She couldn't reject something she'd never been offered. Right?

He cleared his throat and pushed the damp hair off his forehead. "We have to get back. It'll be light soon."

He didn't miss the slight sigh or the little shake of her head. She opened her mouth to speak, but closed it again without saying a word, before she turned and started to walk away from him. When she put her foot down, he heard her suck air through her teeth. She didn't stop, though. She kept going, despite the limp.

He caught up to her. "Glass in your foot?"

She nodded, and Nick scooped her into his arms and strode toward the house.

"Put me down, Nick. Your leg—"

"Relax," was his curt reply. He tried not to smell

the scent of her hair drifting up to him or feel the curve of her hip against his groin. "Just relax." His tone was gentler the second time, and she complied, linking her arms around his neck and resting her head on his shoulder. Nick gave up trying not to notice her—the feel of her in his arms was too much not to notice. The pain in his thigh as he walked back through the woods was minor compared to the exquisite torture this woman was dishing up.

CHAPTER 9

Toni slanted another sidelong glance at Nick. He sat behind the wheel of the parked car beside her, as silent as he'd been for most of the day. His chiseled jaw didn't move except for the occasional twitch. He'd been all business from the moment they'd returned to the hidden apartment. One hundred percent efficient, effective Federal Agent Manelli had taken over. The Nick she'd longed to know, the one she thought she'd finally uncovered, was gone. On the upside, so was the phony thug persona.

With military precision he'd supervised the packing of her things to erase any trace of her presence. He'd gathered a sparse few of his own, including, she noted, the jeans and the high-tops, the basketball and the photograph. He left every one of those expensive suits behind.

Meticulously he'd orchestrated her sister's safe

departure from the country, just the way he wanted to orchestrate her own. She'd come very close to losing that round. But in the end, he'd caved. She was still with him.

He stiffened in anticipation when another set of headlights broke through the darkness. The white beams moved eerily, illuminating his face. They passed, and Toni heard his aggravated sigh. For over an hour they'd been parked there in the nearly empty lot. The only other vehicles there were an abandoned Buick and a stripped-down framework that might once have been a Corvette.

"He should have been here by now." The worry in his voice came through clearly, and Toni longed to comfort him. He'd been so distant since this morning, she wasn't sure she knew how.

She knew he was worried about Carl. That was part of the reason for his icy demeanor. Carl should have been there to meet with him at dusk. It was an arrangement they'd made months ago. If it got to the point where they both had to pull out in a hurry, they'd go their separate ways and meet in this crumbling parking lot at sundown the following night. Nick had told her that. He'd also told her about the drug shipment that had been confiscated the night he'd been shot, and his feeling that Taranto had expected the police raid. He thought Taranto suspected Carl. If he was right, then Carl was in serious danger.

Toni thought of the man's gentle voice and his obvious worry about Nick, and she bit her lip. If

Taranto had him—

Nick glanced again at his watch. He shook his head and looked around the empty parking lot. Change the subject, Toni thought. Get him talking. At least the endless minutes of waiting would tick by a little faster.

"Joey should be safely in her hotel in Orlando by now. It's such a relief knowing she's away from all this."

He looked at her, his eyes narrow, his temper short. "If you had half a brain, you'd be with her."

She shook her head. "I told you, Nick, I have just as much invested here as you do. I'm not walking away until I see it through. If you had put me on the flight out, I'd have caught the next one right back here."

"So you've pointed out—repeatedly. It's the only reason you're here. I couldn't risk you wandering around on your own. Lou would've had you in a matter of hours."

She rolled her eyes. "How *did* I ever manage without you? Must've been pure luck that I didn't bungle my incompetent self into an early grave last year when I took on those drug lords south of the equator."

"I didn't mean...." He shook his head and sighed loudly. "Okay. You're good at this, all right? You're just too damn gutsy for your own good. You rush headlong into situations that could be dangerous. That's all I meant. You're reckless. Not incompetent."

She blinked and looked at him. "Gutsy, huh?"

She felt the frown come and go as she digested that. After a moment she shook her head quickly. "Nah. Katrina's the gutsy one. I could never do the things she does," she said.

"Things like following mob hit men into dark alleys in the middle of the night? Or maybe things like slugging a six-two alleged killer who's carrying a gun because he says something you don't like?" He looked away from her face. "You're gutsy, lady. You wouldn't be doing what you've been doing otherwise."

"You have it all wrong." She answered him quickly, the words tumbling out before she had a chance to think about them. "I do the things I do, to make up for what I didn't do before."

"Before?" His dark brows drew together as he regarded her in the dim interior of the car. "You're talking about your father's suicide, aren't you? Toni, you can't keep blaming yourself for that."

She couldn't hold his gaze. She hadn't understood until recently, the connection between her guilt over her father's suicide and her need to fix society's ills in any way she could. She gazed through the window, seeing nothing. "I knew what was happening. I should have done something."

"You were still in high school. What could you have done?"

"Something. Anything. I shouldn't have let it go on so long. I shouldn't have let him...." She stopped and tried to swallow the lump in her throat.

Nick touched her arm. "You couldn't have

changed what happened, Toni."

"I could. I knew when he left the house that day... it was in his eyes. I shouldn't have let him go."

He was quiet for a long moment. Maybe he finally believed her. Not that it mattered. *She* knew. She'd always known. When he took her chin in his hand and turned her to face him, she wished he'd just drop the subject.

"You know what I think?" Nick asked. She shook her head, and he went on. "I think you feel so guilty about it that you want to be punished. I think that's why you challenge death at every turn. Maybe you're hoping it'll beat you one of these times. Maybe you think, somewhere deep down in that pretty head of yours, that you don't deserve to live when he didn't."

In the dark, quiet car, Nick deftly opened the festering wound in her soul and let the infection begin to heal. Toni felt her lips tremble. She couldn't speak. How could he see so clearly the truth she'd kept hidden from herself for such a long time? The accuracy of what he'd said was so clear to her all at once. Why hadn't she seen it before?

"It wasn't your fault, Toni." He watched the changes in her face for a moment. "Do you think your father would've wanted you to spend your life paying for his decision that day?"

She shook her head. "No, but—"

"You know how bad you've felt since he took his own life?" His arms suddenly encircled her shoulders. He brought her close to him, until she was held like a child. "That's how bad your sister would feel if you followed his example. Do you want to be responsible for causing her that kind of pain?"

She shook her head hard, moving it against his shoulder where it was cradled. "No! I never meant...I didn't realize..." She released all her breath at once. She felt like crying. The huge burden she'd been bearing for so long suddenly grew lighter. It didn't vanish; some of it remained. For the first time in a very long time, though, she thought she understood it. God. This changed the scope of her very existence! She felt free all of a sudden.

She sat up slightly and studied his face in awed fascination. "You should have been a shrink. My God, how do you see so much?"

He shrugged. One hand stroked a wisp of hair away from her face. "You're getting to be a little bit transparent to me. Maybe because we've been together constantly for the past week. Maybe because I've wrestled with a lot of the same demons myself. For a long time I blamed myself for not being able to save my brother. So I know you. I know you on a level I think few people ever know another. Except..."

"Except what?"

He released her and settled back in his seat. Toni settled back, too, but close enough so their bodies touched. "Did you ever want to do anything else?" he asked. "I mean, besides write tell-all books to clear your conscience?"

She allowed a small smile. "I love to write and I'm good at it."

"I'll let you know after I read your latest book."

She smiled fully. Finally the easy, relaxed atmosphere between them had returned. "I had a plan, you know. A long time ago before, I got so wrapped up in being a crime fighter."

He folded his arms, clasping his hands behind his head. "Tell me."

Toni closed her eyes and envisioned the life she'd allowed to exist only in her dreams. "Rural town," she told him. "Not suburban, *rural.* I'm not even sure my road is paved. The house is a rambling old Victorian—white with black shutters and huge open porches. I have a big office with a window that overlooks the enormous back lawn. There are yellow roses growing there and a flowering crab apple tree. I write wonderful books with happy endings. When I get tired of sitting at the computer, I walk the dog."

She didn't need to look at him to know his brows shot up. "The dog?"

"Um-hmm. He's a huge gray-and-white sheepdog. He's so shaggy I have to trim the hair around his eyes every few weeks so he can see. His name is Ralph. We walk together every day, down the path to the duck pond, and—"

"This is one vivid plan," he said slowly.

"I'm a writer. I live to fill in the details."

Headlights approached once more, and Nick sat up straighter. This time the oncoming car veered into the parking lot and pulled up alongside. The driver's window lowered slowly. The man sitting there was not Carl.

"My boss," Nick muttered, then lowered his

window. "Harry, what the hell's going on?"

The white haired man in the other car met Nick's gaze, all but ignoring Toni's presence. "It isn't good, Manelli. Carl's dropped off the radar. No one's been able to find a trace of him."

Nick flinched as if he'd been struck. The man in the other car kept on speaking. He glanced at Toni. "Her sister didn't show for her flight, Nick. We haven't been able to locate her, either."

"Damn."

Toni shook her head rapidly. "No. It isn't what you're thinking. I know my sister. She probably just set her heels and decided she wasn't leaving. When I talked to her earlier and explained the situation—" she swallowed and cleared her throat "—I should have known she agreed too easily. She's stubborn as a mule sometimes."

"Must run in the family," Nick muttered under his breath.

"I hope you're right," Harry said. He returned his attention to Nick. "Why's she still with you, Manelli? You had orders—"

"She would have come right back and become a target," Nick said. "It was safer to keep her with me."

"I'd appreciate it if you two would stop talking as if I'm not here." Toni looked at Nick, feeling a dark terror creep into her heart. If Taranto had her sister...

"What do we do now?" she asked.

Harry reworded her question and put it to Nick. "Do you have enough on Taranto to make an arrest stick?"

Nick shook his head. "He paid me to kill Toni—but that's no good because I don't have enough to prove it and Toni isn't dead. He sent me to witness Vinnie's hit, but he never really confessed to that on tape. The man knows enough to talk in circles. He says all he needs to say without ever admitting a thing." He looked down and shook his head.

"What kind of evidence do you need?" Toni asked.

Both men looked at her, and Nick said, "What kind have you *got*?"

She did a mental inventory of the evidence she'd gathered while researching her book, trying to think of the most damning. "I have photographs of Lou Taranto passing a large manila envelope to a man named Santos. Santos was later arrested in Colombia for murder."

"Right," Harry interrupted. "Last year. He'd tampered with the plane that was supposed to carry Juan Perez to the U.S. to stand trial for drug trafficking. The plane crashed after takeoff. Perez died, along with the three DEA agents who were escorting him back."

"Juan Perez was Lou Taranto's cocaine supplier in Colombia," Nick said.

Toni nodded. "That's right. And if he'd made it here to stand trial, he might have been offered a deal in exchange for his testimony against Taranto. Santos took that envelope from Lou and left for Colombia within six hours. And when he got there, a large amount of money suddenly appeared in his bank account."

"Toni, how the hell do you know all this?"

She met Nick's intense look. "I followed Lou for weeks researching this book. One day I saw him meet with Santos in a little cafe. I slipped the waitress fifty bucks for her apron and got close enough to eavesdrop. Took the shots of Taranto passing Santos the envelope, and they never even glanced up at me. When they left the diner, I decided to follow Santos and the envelope instead of Lou. That's how I know he went straight to Colombia. I still had connections down there from the last book and I called one of them. Larry Wetzel. He has a lucrative little investigations agency going down there. He'll testify if you force him to. Anyway, he met the flight and tailed Santos on that end. He reported that Santos had checked into a motel and got himself a job at a small airfield. The next day Perez's plane took off from that same airfield and crashed."

Nick stared at her and shook his head. "Slipped the waitress fifty bucks..." he muttered, more to himself than anyone else.

"How much of this is documented?" Harry seemed eager.

"The photograph of Lou handing Santos the envelope is irrefutable. I have another one of Santos boarding the flight to Colombia. You already have proof that Santos sabotaged the Perez's flight. He would've been tried for that last year if he hadn't been found hanging by the neck in his cell."

"If that was self-inflicted, I'll eat my badge," Harry said softly.

"Still, it's not solid," Nick put it

"I have the envelope. There's a coffee stain on it, identical to the one that shows in the first photo. My PI friend grabbed it out of a trash can where Santos had dropped it after lighting a match to it. Larry managed to douse the flame before it did too much damage."

Nick looked at Harry, then at Toni again. "Come on, *Katrina,* don't keep us in suspense. What was inside?"

She couldn't help smiling a little smugly. "A five-by-seven glossy of Perez, and a handwritten note with the name of the airfield, the flight number and the time and date of departure. The only thing that wasn't there was the money, and that is still in Santos's bank account."

Harry's long, low whistle came at the same moment that Nick asked, "Where is all this evidence?" She didn't answer. His hands clasped her shoulders, and he squeezed them between his fingers. "Don't play games, Toni. Tell me."

She shook her head. "I'll take you to it." He frowned, and his grip tightened, but she only stuck her chin out a little farther. "If I tell you, you'll try to stash me somewhere while you go after it alone."

His hands fell to his sides. He nodded. "That's right." He glanced downward for a long moment, then faced her again. "Your apartment. That locked room, right?"

She shook her head, but not before he'd seen the answer in her eyes. His gaze pummeled her. "All right, yes. But you don't know the combination for my safe, and I won't give it to you."

"I'll get into it whether you give me the combination or not."

"But that'll take time. Isn't time of the essence here?"

"She's got you there, Manelli," Harry interrupted. "Take her along, we're wasting time arguing. I'll get a team in place outside her building. You'll have backup. One hour."

Nick glared from Toni to Harry. "I don't like it—she'll be a moving target."

"We'll take precautions," Harry told him. "Beginning right now. Get out of the car." Nick hesitated. "Come on, Manelli, I don't have all night. You've been driving that one through this entire operation. Taranto knows it. We'll switch. I'll get that thing out of sight for a while. You two wearing vests?"

"Not yet," Nick said.

"There's a pair in my back seat. Get into them." Harry got out of the car as he spoke and yanked Nick's door open. "Come on, let's not sit here all night."

Toni could see that Nick didn't want to comply, but the moment he opened his mouth to argue the other man held up a hand. "Consider it an order."

Lou Taranto leaned back in his overstuffed chair. He took the cigarette from his lips and held it in front of him, studying the smoke that spiraled up from the glowing tip. He released what he'd inhaled, and his face became a blur in the center of the stark room. Viper stood at his right hand, his button eyes gleaming. He alternately clenched and opened his red-knuckled hand.

"Bring him around," Taranto ordered.

"He's had it, Lou." Viper thumbed one of Carl's swollen, purple eyelids open and let it fall. The only things holding Carl upright were the ropes that bound him to the straight wooden chair. "He's told you all he's gonna."

"He's told me nothing. But he will, damn lousy cop. Bring him around!"

"I told you, he's had it. Damn near comatose. Be dead in a few hours."

"Stubborn little son of a bitch," Lou muttered.

Viper rolled his eyes. "You don't need Salducci to tell you what you already know. Nick's a cop, too. It's obvious. They came in right around the same time. They were both in on the shipment that was taken."

"Nicky took a bullet that night!"

"And Carl patched him up. You know he's a Fed. You think he'd have patched up my leg? Yours? No way. He'd have smiled while we bled to death. What do you need? A signed confession? Manelli's a cop. I say we off him."

Lou came to his feet as fast as his ample weight would allow and gripped Viper by the lapels. "We gotta make sure, you little twit, because of the girl! If Nicky's a cop, then you can bet your skinny ass she ain't dead. She's still out there and she's got more on us than any cop does. We gotta find out for sure."

"She saw my face," Viper ground out, jerking himself from Lou's hands. "And so did he. I'm on the line here, and I'll deal with it my way."

"Don't cross me, Viper, or I—"

"Don't you worry, Lou. I'll handle it. You'll thank me before this is over." Viper spun and left the room. Lou opened the door and bellowed after him, but he kept on walking. A moment later his car left the lot outside the Century.

A bulky man with a crew cut loomed over Lou a moment later. "Cops are on the way, boss. Our insider says they got warrants to search the place. What do we do?"

Lou looked at the limp, bruised man in the chair. "Cop or not, Nicky didn't know who that broad was until I told him, I'd bet my life on it."

The overgrown hulk in front of him puckered his brows. "Huh?"

Lou turned, paced away from him, muttering to himself. "If he's a cop, he'll go to her apartment to see what she had on me. If he's loyal, he'll go because I told him to." He stopped in front of Carl and lifted the lax head by a tuft of hair. "What do you suppose he'll think when he finds you there waitin' for him, huh Salducci?"

"I don't get it, boss."

Lou yanked a small notepad from his shirt pocket and scribbled three letters onto the first sheet, then tore it off. "Here, pin this to his chest. Then take him to the Rio broad's apartment and dump him there."

"But how can I get him in there without somebody seein' him?"

"How the hell do I know? Roll him in a rug for all I care, just do it! We'll soon find out just how loyal Nick Manelli is to the family."

Harry Anderson shook his head slowly and tried to see it again in his mind. The way that small woman stuck her chin in Nick's face and told him what was what—the way he *let her!* He'd finally met his match, the big jerk. It was about time.

He drove Nick's car toward the gloomy mansion they'd set him up in. He'd retrieve the backup drives with the surveillance footage on them, just in case the del Rio girl couldn't produce what she said she could. They'd be better than nothing. At the very least, they could be used to identify Viper. Then he'd head back to headquarters and get a team together to back Nick up when he went to the woman's apartment. Taranto would be watching, if Harry's opinion was worth anything.

He was within sight of those ridiculous iron gates, rounding a bend in the curving road, when he heard glass shatter and felt searing pain at his left temple. He clenched the wheel reflexively, jerking it to the right, and felt the front tires leave the pavement. Then he was airborne and heading down the steep drop alongside the road. He prayed the bullet that had hit him would kill him before he hit bottom.

CHAPTER 10

Nick circled the block twice, then turned to enter the parking garage. He drove slowly beneath the fluorescent tube lights on the low ceiling, scanning every vehicle, peering around every support column. The place seemed as still as a graveyard. The hair on the back of his neck bristled in anticipation. He could feel that he was being watched. His fear made him more careful than he'd ever been. Not fear for himself, but for the woman in the seat beside him, crouched low as he'd instructed. He was afraid he'd lose her. The cycle had repeated itself again today, just in case he'd forgotten the way things worked. Taranto had Carl. There was a grim certainty in Nick's gut that he wouldn't see his best friend again.

He nearly drove past the stairwell, he was so focused on seeing into every shadowy recess. He pulled up close to the heavy door, shut the car off, pocketed the keys. It'll be all right, he told himself.

Harry must have a half-dozen men in the building, a dozen more outside, if he was true to form. Nothing could happen to Toni. He wouldn't let it.

He opened the door and stood for a moment, every sense attuned. He saw no one, heard nothing but the normal traffic noises and a car squealing on a level below. The place smelled of exhaust and hot pavement. He glanced down at Toni, nodding once. She slid across the seat and got out his door, staying bent low, just the way he'd instructed. With his body blocking her from view on one side, the car on the other, she hurried to the open door of the stairwell. Her running shoes made no sound. She moved through the doorway, pressed her back against the inside wall and waited. Nick closed the car door and moved in beside her. He pulled the heavy stairwell door closed. The place echoed like an empty church. If anyone opened the door, he'd hear them. Then again, anyone already here would hear him, too. Any sound would echo through the cool, hollow stairway. He pressed a finger to his lips to remind Toni of that.

He pulled his weapon from the holster under his left arm, held it barrel-up, and began to move up the stairs, keeping Toni close behind him. His caution doubled when he reached a landing. He pushed her flat to the wall behind her and peeked around to the next flight, taking his time to be sure it was safe before urging her to come along. It seemed to take forever to reach the fourth floor. In reality, it took less than ten minutes.

Nick glanced through the small square of glass, criss-crossed with wire between the panes, before he opened the door and stepped into a tiled corridor. Toni came out behind him. Her tug on his jacket brought his gaze around fast. She frowned at the gun in his hand and shook her head. Okay, she was probably right. He'd draw some attention sneaking through the corridors of an apartment building with an automatic in his hand. He slipped it back inside his jacket.

Trying to walk causally through the hall was the toughest thing he'd done in a long time. Moving steadily beneath the lighted ceiling panels, between the doors that lined both sides—doors that might swing open at any second to reveal a hard-faced man with an automatic.

He swallowed. It wouldn't happen that way. Taranto still trusted him. Carl wouldn't talk, no matter what they did. Besides, Harry was here, somewhere, with an armed entourage.

They came to a T and went left. Three doors down, they stopped in front of Toni's apartment. Their gazes locked for a moment, and that unspoken *thing* passed between them—that connection he couldn't acknowledge and didn't recognize.

He pulled his gaze away and looked at the door, taking out his gun. Toni was quicker, already lifting her key to the lock. But when she touched the door, it fell open without a sound, and she jerked away from it, eyes wide. It hadn't been locked. It hadn't even been closed properly. Someone had been there.

Maybe they still were. He pushed her to the wall and mouthed the word, "Wait," then let his gun lead him into the apartment.

His stomach clenched when he saw Carl in the middle of the floor. He wasn't sure he'd have recognized him except for the familiar clothes he wore. A slip of paper on his jacket had the word "Cop" penciled on it. His face varied in shades of crimson, blue and purple. His eyes looked like two fat grapes. From the looks of it, he would never open them again. There was no doubt in Nick's mind that Carl was dead. His training helped him push his paralyzing grief aside, allowing only the cold certainty that Lou Taranto would pay dearly to remain. He let the experience of years on the job take over and quickly checked each room of the apartment. When he was certain no one else was there, he went back to tell Toni it was safe to come inside.

She already had. She was on the floor beside Carl, tucking a blanket around him. Nick recognized the throw that had been on the couch and then the matching pillows she'd placed under his friend's feet.

"We have to get him to a hospital, Nick." Toni's voice trembled.

Nick looked to see that she'd already closed the door, then he knelt opposite her, over Carl. He couldn't believe his eyes when Carl shook his head slightly left and right. "No...hospital."

"Jesus, he's alive."

Nick's gut twisted and guilt flooded in, right behind the rush of relief. This had been *his* obsession.

It should have been *him* lying on the floor, *his* face encrusted with dried blood, barely able to form a single word. It should have been him, not Carl.

The battered lips moved again. "Nick?"

Nick gripped his friend's shoulders to let him know he was there. Carl couldn't open his eyes to see for himself. "I'm right here, pal."

"Lou... watch—watching," Carl managed. His slurred speech had Nick more worried about brain damage than about Lou.

"To see if I help you," Nick finished for him. A white rage unfurled inside him.

"We should call an ambulance," Toni whispered.

The tightness in her voice brought Nick's gaze back to hers. There were tears brimming in her eyes. She leaned closer to Carl, keeping her voice soothingly low and soft. "We're going to take care of you," she was telling him. "You'll be okay."

It reminded Nick of the way she'd spoken to him the night before, when the fire in his thigh had burned bright. Funny, he'd barely felt the pain since arriving in this building. Adrenaline was a great anesthetic. "If Lou's watching, Toni, he doesn't intend to let Carl out of here alive. There's no way he'll let an ambulance crew into the building." Frustration gnawed at him. He had to think! Carl needed serious help and he needed it fast.

"Didn't...tell...him," Carl stammered, "anything."

"I never thought otherwise. And I know what you're getting at. My cover's intact. You're thinking I should leave you here and keep it that way. I'm not going to do that, so shut up and let me think."

Nick felt Carl's hand close around his with surprising force. "He'll...kill you...both."

"Not if I can help it, he won't. And if we can get out of here in one piece, he's going down. Turns out Toni had the goods on him all along." He glanced up at Toni. "Get that evidence, will you?"

Nodding, she got up and hurried into the room that was her office. He heard her moving around in there at the same time he heard the apartment door opening. He yanked his gun out. The door swung open and Nick saw the barrel of a .44 Magnum staring him in the face. There was a small blond woman attached to it. She seemed vaguely familiar.

"What the hell—"

"Put that gun down and tell me what you've done with my sister, or I'm gonna splatter you to hell and gone!"

Nick realized who she was. Somehow he wasn't surprised. He lowered his gun slowly and laid it on the carpet. "Come on in and close the door."

Toni chose that moment to emerge from the office with a thick folder in her hands. The two women spied each other at the same moment, and a second later both the .44 and file folder were on the floor as they embraced.

"You've had me worried to death," the blonde accused. "Are you all right?"

"Fine." They pulled apart, and Toni seemed to drink in her sister's face. "I'm so glad you're okay. When they said you didn't get on that flight, I—"

"You didn't expect me to just fly off and leave when you were in trouble, did you?"

Toni shook her head. "Not really. Where on earth did you get that cannon?"

Joey glanced down at the gun on the floor, then at the man who lay barely alive a few feet past it. "My God, what happened?"

"He's a federal agent, sis. They both are. Taranto found out."

"How did you get into the building?" Nick asked when there was finally a long enough break.

"Through the front entrance. Why?"

Nick blew a sigh and shook his head. "This is a real high-security place you picked, Toni. What the hell do you do with all that money your books earn you?"

"She hoards it away like a pack rat," her sister inserted with a mock scowl. "Saving it for some rambling Victorian house and a sheepdog." She glanced at Nick and offered him a tremulous smile. "Thanks for keeping her alive to spend it."

There was affection in her pretty eyes. "Nick Manelli," he told her.

"Josephine Bradshaw. Sorry about the gun before." Joey looked again at Carl on the floor. "Shouldn't he be on his way to a hospital?"

"Taranto is watching," Nick told her. If we try to take him out of here, there's a chance we'll get him killed."

She frowned and shook her head. "What are you going to do?"

"I haven't figured that out yet."

"I have," Toni said.

Nick looked at her fast. He hadn't liked the slight waver in her voice, and he saw now the unnatural paleness in her cheeks. She was scared. "Tell me. I can see you don't think I'm going to like it."

"Doesn't matter if you like it. Carl needs help, Nick, or he won't make it. So we're gonna give Taranto exactly the show he's expecting. I'll wrap myself up in a blanket. You can carry me down to the car, and we'll leave. Taranto will think I'm Carl and come after us. You just said he wouldn't let Carl make it to a hospital alive. He'll come after *us*. When he does, it will be safe for my sister to get Carl to an emergency room."

Nick rose from Carl's side, took Toni's shoulders in his hands and gazed into her bottomless eyes. "Listen close, Toni Rio, 'cause I'm only saying this once. No. It isn't going to happen."

She stood straighter. "Then I assume you have a better idea?" Her chin jutted, and her eyes flashed with determination that overrode her fear. "We'll be all right, Nick. You know your boss Harry and all his men are out there somewhere. They'll be right behind Taranto when he comes after us. We'll be fine."

His hands tightened. "You're offering to act as a decoy, Toni. A target. What am I supposed to do if Taranto manages to catch us? Stand there and watch him give the order to put a bullet in your head?"

"Are our chances any better by staying here? They

aren't and you know it. The longer we argue about this, the closer Carl gets to having no chance at all."

Carl moaned low as if to punctuate her words. His body shuddered once, then went still. Joey tensed beside him, pressing the pads of her fingers to his throat. She sighed and took them away. "Toni's right. He can't stay here. Every minute is pushing him closer to death."

"We'll leave the evidence here," Toni said quickly. "Joey can give it to Harry when he gets to the hospital."

Nick shook his head. *"You* give it to Harry. I'll try and lead Taranto away myself."

"If you do, Nick, I'll get in Joey's car and come after you."

He closed his eyes slowly, opened them again. He felt like a projectile had lodged in his chest. She was offering him a way to save Carl, his best friend since he'd been no more than a smart-mouth kid. Carl— whom he loved. But Toni's offer put her at risk. Toni, the woman who'd handed him the ammunition to put Taranto away. Toni—whom he...what?

He damn well didn't love her. It would be stupid to love a woman he knew he'd lose in the end. Stupid!

"You wanna tell me why you're being so stubborn about this?"

Her gaze held his as a magnet holds steel. "You'll have twice the chance of getting away if I'm with you, Nick. Look, this might be your case—your vendetta, but it's my evidence. Whether you like it or not, we're in this together. I'm not going to walk away and let you take the heat alone just because things are starting to get dangerous. Taranto might not follow you if you leave alone."

Carl began to shake again, violently this time, his legs stiffening as his heels jostled off the pillows and tapped a beat on the floor. Toni pulled from Nick's restraining hands, disappeared into the bedroom and returned a second later with a blanket draped over her shoulders. She bent to pick up the gun her sister had dropped.

Joey got to her feet, wrapped Toni in her arms and squeezed. "Be careful."

To his shock, Joey stepped away from her sister and turned to fold him in a powerful embrace. "I'll take care of Carl. Don't worry about him. And don't keep questioning yourself the way you've been doing. You're right, this is risky. But it's also the only way."

Nick frowned, sending Toni a questioning look.

"Trust her, Nick. My sister knows things."

Toni had to remain limp in Nick's arms as he carried her through the corridors and into the chill of the stairwell. She'd much rather have wound her arms around his neck and hidden her face against him. Shivers of pure fear rushed through her when she thought about what they were doing, so she tried not to think about it. There was no alternative, no way she could've stayed behind. Her feelings for Nick had grown very powerful, very quickly. The thought of staying behind and allowing him to face this alone had been unacceptable. She hadn't been able to consider it.

She told herself that it was because he'd done something so precious to her by making her see what had driven her all this time. Recognizing that the emotion behind her recklessness had been a form of survivor's guilt over her father's suicide was a major step toward overcoming it. He'd opened the shutters, spilling brilliant light in the shadowy corners of her mind, and forcing her to see what was there. Now she could begin to sweep away the cobwebs and dust that had built up for so long. She owed him for that.

Still, there was more than gratitude in her heart. She recognized that he had some musty, sealed-off rooms in his mind, too. Rooms he rarely allowed himself to enter. She knew the wound in his soul he'd allowed to fester since his brother's death. She knew that being abandoned by his parents had injured him deeply, and she knew he refused to admit that. She wanted to help him clean out those cluttered rooms and then fill them with warmth and happiness.

It was amazing how well she'd come to know Nick in such a short time. It hit her hardest whenever he looked into her eyes. It was palpable, whatever passed between them then—as if they were touching souls. She wondered if he felt it, too. He kept himself so closed off, it was hard to tell.

She felt his body tense and shook herself. They were at the entrance to the parking garage. As he carried her through the doorway, she tensed, but he moved fast, lowering her onto the passenger seat faster than she would have believed possible. She kept the blanket over her face, let her body sag limply to one side, and clutched the textured walnut grips of the huge handgun he'd given her. He was behind the wheel in an instant, gunning the motor and speeding away. She knew when they left the underground garage and turned onto the street

"Is anyone following—" She began to sit up a little as she spoke and flipped the blanket away from her face. Nick pushed her down again. Her backside was on the seat, but her head was pressed to his rib cage. He held her for a moment, his arm around her like a steel band.

When it came away, she saw him adjust the rearview. "Oh, yeah. They're coming, all right. Where the hell is Harry with our backup?"

Toni felt the car jerk and heard the squeal of the tires when he took a sharp corner, then another. She wished she could see his face. She heard the grim tone in his voice, though. "No cops. No sign of Harry. I can't believe this!" He took another corner, drew a breath. "Something must've happened to him before he could get back to HQ. I think we're on our own."

Toni tried to make her voice level. "What—what could've happened to him?"

"Don't worry about it now. Listen, I'm going to take a few quick turns, see if I can lose them for a second. Just long enough for you to get out. Slide over by the door and get ready—"

"I told you we're in this together, Nick."

"That was when we thought we had backup."

"And now I'm the only backup you have," she countered. "I'm not going anywhere."

He drove in stony silence then, never slowing down, his muscles tense. Suddenly he hit the brakes, and she heard him swear viciously. His thigh went rigid under her hand, and she lifted her head very slightly to see what had caused him to skid to a halt.

A car had pulled across the street in front of them. Nick shifted into reverse and slammed the pedal to the floor, turning the wheel sharply. He was crossways in the street when a van skidded to a stop behind them. They were trapped. The only way out was a narrow channel between the vehicles. It would take them over the sidewalk and smack into a mailbox, but—

Before Toni could complete the thought, Taranto's men were out of their vehicles and Nick was pressing down onto the seat and tugging the blanket over her head. She glimpsed two rifles pointing toward them from behind the car. A frantic glance to her right showed two more from the van.

Lou Taranto's voice came clearly. "Out of the car, Nicky. I don't have time to play with you. I count three and put a bullet in the gas tank. You don't wanna go out like that. Get out and take it like a man."

Nick looked down at her, into her eyes, and again she felt that powerful surge of some force linking them together. "Stay down low," he instructed. His voice was deep and soft. "They still think it's Carl in here, half dead, maybe all the way. They won't be expecting it. You count to ten, then shift into gear and put the pedal to the floor." His eyes shifted, indicating the same escape route she'd recognized.

She frowned. "I don't under—" She stopped, eyes widening when she saw his hand close around the door handle. "No. Nick, you can't go out there!"

"He means it, Toni. He'll blow us both to hell if I don't." He reached down, threading his fingers in her hair. "Their attention will be on me. When I get far enough from the car, floor it. It's your only chance."

"No. I won't do it, you can't—"

"Manelli! I'm taking aim! Get out now or burn!"

Nick blinked. He leaned over and touched her face with his lips. "Do it. Don't look back." He forced a lopsided grin. "For what it's worth, Toni, it meant something with you. It never did before. Not once."

He wrenched the door open and got out fast. Toni barely restrained herself from shrieking at him, lunging after him, grabbing him by the shirt and pulling him back into the car. She slid herself into his spot behind the wheel, still keeping her head low enough so they couldn't see from outside.

"Move away from the car," Taranto yelled.

Toni watched through the side mirrors as Nick walked slowly toward the rear of the car, then past it. He stood several yards behind the vehicle, and as he'd predicted, every gun was trained on him. She swallowed hard. This couldn't be happening. She blinked and when she opened her eyes, she saw a man coming toward the passenger side, his gun drawn and ready.

"If Salducci isn't dead yet, finish him." Taranto's voice echoed in her mind. She turned herself in the seat so she faced that door. She pulled the blanket around her, leaving a crack she could see through and poking the six-inch nickel barrel through another. She thumbed the safety off.

The car door opened, and the tall, dark outline of a man filled it. She watched in horror as his gun barrel lowered toward her. And then she tightened her finger on the trigger, and the big gun bucked violently in her hands. The roar of it was deafening in the car's interior. The man reacted as if he'd been slammed in the chest with a hammer, jerking backward. His face went lax and his body sank limply to the ground.

She had to act fast while the confusion lasted. At the moment, they must think the thug's gun was the one they'd heard. She jammed her finger on the trunk-release button and shifted the car into reverse, backing up so fast she left rubber and hitting the brakes only when she was about to run Nick over. Gunfire erupted, and the car sank with Nick's body weight as he threw himself into the open trunk. The window to her left exploded, showering her with glass, but she stomped the gas and sped away, hitting the mailbox hard enough to rattle her teeth, jumping the curb and squealing over a stretch of sidewalk. The car dropped back to the street again on the other side of the parked van, and Toni pushed the pedal to the floor. She couldn't believe how close the gunshots were! It felt as if those thugs were in the damn car with her!

The lights around her blended into a single blurred haze. The traffic sounds became a buzzing drone as adrenaline surged. They must be chasing her. She couldn't see them now, but they must be. Was Nick hit? Was he even now bleeding to death in the trunk? She'd killed a man. The weight of it dropped on her suddenly and powerfully. She'd taken a life. She hadn't even known him and she'd killed him. Her stomach heaved, and she bit her lip until she drew blood to fight off the nausea. Tears pooled in her eyes, and no amount of blinking prevented them spilling over. She'd never been so frightened in her life! Her hands shook, partly from the force with which she gripped the wheel and partly from the remnants of her terror. She could barely see where she drove now, but she kept the pressure on the accelerator all the same...

...until she careened into an intersection and heard the blast of an air horn. The impact snapped her head back. She heard grinding, bending metal and shattering glass. She smelled diesel smoke and hot rubber. She felt a warm trickle at her temple and then she felt nothing at all.

CHAPTER 11

Toni opened her eyes and blinked her vision into focus. The floor where she lay smelled musty. The room exuded chill dampness. She knew it was a basement before she realized the floor was packed earth or the walls, chipped cinder block.

"About time, Manelli. I been waitin' all damn day."

The cold voice came from near the center of the room and drew Toni's gaze. She barely stopped herself from gasping when she saw Nick in a straight-backed wooden chair. A rope lashed around his ankles kept his feet immobile. She thought another must be holding his wrists together behind the chair's back, but she couldn't see for certain, despite the glaring bare light bulb that dangled from the end of a frayed cord, over his head.

Lou Taranto stood a few feet in front of Nick, facing him. Viper was at his side. Nick's eyes seemed glazed, and Toni vaguely remembered the crash.

Someone rushing over to her, opening her car door, and jabbing her in the arm with something. She remembered looking behind the car for Nick, certain he'd been in the trunk. And she'd spotted him lying on the pavement, a guy in a suit bent over him, injecting him with a needle.

They'd both been drugged. She had no idea how long ago or where they might be now.

"You disappointed me, Nicky. I trusted you. Like my own son, I trusted you, but you betrayed me." Lou released a short shot of air. "A Fed! A lousy, freaking Fed—don't bother denying it. No one fools Lou Taranto for long."

Nick wasn't looking at him. His gaze probed the corners of the room, and Toni realized that with the bright light on him and the shadows everywhere else, he couldn't see her. He searched for her, squinting hard. She wanted to call out to him, but didn't dare. It might be better to stay quiet for a few minutes. She might get an idea that could help if she could watch them while they thought she was still unconscious.

Viper raised his fist and delivered a shocking blow to the side of Nick's head. The chair toppled to the floor with Nick in it, and Toni damn near jumped to her feet and charged the little weasel. A small voice from within warned her it would do more harm than good. What she needed was a weapon.

Viper leaned over, righted the chair with a rough jerk. "Pay attention when the boss is talkin' to you, Manelli. Lou has a few things to get off his chest." He leaned closer. "And then it's my turn. You know how your pal Salducci looked when you found him? He looked good compared to what you're gonna look like, Nicky boy. You're gonna die slow."

"Big talk's easy when I'm tied up and drugged, isn't it?" Nick's voice came out even and low. "Untie me and say it again, you little prick."

"Talk all you want, Manelli. You're a dead man. I don't pay much attention to dead men."

"I'm not dead yet."

Viper smiled, and it sent a chill right down Toni's spine. "Yeah, you are."

Toni reached out in the darkness, patting the damp dirt floor with her hands. They hadn't tied her as they had Nick. They must not consider her much of a threat. She strained her eyes to see in the darkness. A rickety wooden door hung at one side of the room. An ancient, molding pile of firewood was stacked in a corner. A broken wood crate, with a few dust-covered shapes in its bottom sat beside a rusted water tank that had long since toppled onto its side. A weapon. She needed a weapon. A length of pipe, a hammer, anything!

"I need to know what they have on me, Nicky." Lou picked up the conversation again. "The warrant says murder one. What are they basing it on?"

Nick shook his head. "My case was narcotics. The murder rap came from a separate investigation."

Viper hit him again, a straight-on drive of knuckles into his face. The chair slammed over backward, hitting the floor hard. Blood spurted from Nick's nose. Toni heard him cough and spit. Viper yanked the chair upright again by grabbing Nick's shirt in both fists.

Toni rose slowly to her feet, fists clenched so hard her nails pierced her palms. In silence, she looked around her, still cloaked in the darkness. She edged slowly along the cool wall, trying to work her way to the woodpile. A log, if she could find one that wasn't completely rotten, would be good enough to split Viper's skull, she decided.

"Come on, Nicky. You can do better than that," Lou said. "Where's the evidence the Rio broad had on me?"

"If she had anything on you, it's still in her apartment."

"Bullshit. I sent men back there, once we searched your car. Place was empty. No Salducci, no evidence."

Nick shook his head. "I don't know what to tell you, Lou. I called the case as soon as I knew you were onto Salducci. We were packing it in. It wasn't my problem any more."

"You're lying!"

Nick shrugged, lifting his chin and glaring at Viper. "Isn't that your cue?"

Viper slugged him in the belly this time, and Toni wondered how he kept from vomiting. The chair jumped with the force of the blow. Nick bent as much as the ropes would allow, dragging air into his lungs.

"How am I gonna prepare my defense if I don't know what the evidence is?" Lou spoke in a smooth, friendly tone. "Come on, Nicky, I can't let the business I spent my whole life building go up in smoke like this. I need to know. You're gonna talk eventually. Why put yourself through any more pain when you're just delaying the inevitable?" There was the tiniest waver in his voice. Toni heard it and knew it for what it was—desperation. A weapon, at last.

She stepped out of the darkness, forcing her face to appear composed, emotionless. If they knew what it did to her to see them hurting Nick, it would be over in no time. Her heart felt torn wide open and raw at the pain she knew he must be feeling.

And suddenly, she realized with blinding clarity that she loved him. The pure power of the emotion awed her. She'd had no idea how strong her feelings had become until she'd been forced to see him suffer.

She drew on that strength, closed off the frightened, trembling part of her mind and focused on the strength. There—in one of those corridors within—she met an old friend, clasped her hand, and stood a little straighter. *Help me through this, Katrina.*

Haven't I always? I am you. Or hadn't you figured that out yet?

Toni blinked away the odd sensation and lifted her chin. They hadn't seen her yet. She could back into the shadows and play dead, if she wanted to.

She didn't want to.

"He's telling you the truth, Taranto," she said, loud and clear. "It wasn't his investigation that turned up the evidence against you. It was mine."

All eyes turned in her direction. Toni had to force her gaze not to linger on Nick's bruising, bloody face. If she looked at him, she'd break down and cry. She'd throw her arms around him and kiss the pain away. She'd claw Viper's heart out for hurting him.

"Toni, don't—" Viper hit him again. The skin of his cheek split.

Everything in her wanted to look away, cover her eyes, gag and cry and plead. Instead, she kept her eyes on them and her voice ice cold. "Fine, you don't want to listen to me, that's fine. You finish your little game with Manelli and want to talk, let me know. By then it'll be too late to do anything about it, but it's your loss." Turning at last, she took a step toward her shadowy corner.

"Just a minute, bitch," Lou snapped.

She didn't face him, just stopped moving and blinked rapidly to erase any trace of moisture from her eyes. "If you want my help, you'll have to address me in some other tone, Taranto. I don't answer to 'bitch.'"

His chuckle filled the damp room, reaching all the way to the wooden two-by-six crosspieces supporting the ceiling and the thick cobwebs that covered them. "Viper," he said.

The weasel's clammy hands were clasped around her arms a second later, jerking her around to face Taranto and then holding them pinned to her sides. Nick strained against his bonds. She tried to send him a message with her eyes, but he continued struggling.

Her voice sounding unfamiliar to her own ears, she said, "You don't need to pound on my face to get the information you want, Taranto. I'm no cop.

I'm in this game for one reason and one reason only. Money."

Lou's head came up. "You want to make a deal?" He laughed again. "This one's bold as brass, isn't she?" His gaze shifted from Viper, who held her, to Toni again. "You got nothing to deal with, lady writer. You tell me what I want to know here and now, or I let Viper have an hour alone with you."

Viper bent his head and closed his teeth on Toni's earlobe. It was no playful nibble. He bit hard, intending to hurt her, and he did. She sucked air through her clenched teeth and fought the pain. He let her ear go, and it throbbed angrily. He still kept her arms pulled painfully behind her. "I'm gonna like this, Lou. When can we start?"

Toni forced a smile and then laughter. "You've got to be kidding me! I thought you were a businessman."

"Tell me what you know, sugar."

"I'll tell you a little. The murder charges on you are for the deaths of your ex-supplier and the two DEA agents who were escorting him back to the U.S. You remember Juan Perez, don't you? Your supplier in Colombia? He was the last man who refused the deal I offered. I brought him to his knees and I'll do the same to you."

Lou frowned. "You offered Perez a deal?"

"Before the book went to print I offered to leave certain specifics out if he'd pay me well for my trouble." She shrugged. "He thought I was bluffing." She met Taranto's eyes and felt an icy hand close over her heart. "A lot of men make that mistake. My book brought his entire operation down. The new one's gonna do the same for you. And you wanna know why?"

"This I gotta hear," Lou said. But he wasn't as cocky. Trying to be, but Toni saw through it. She was shaking him.

"Because the pen is mightier than the sword. That's why." He frowned, either because he'd never heard the expression or more likely, didn't understand it. "In more modern terms, my keyboard is more powerful than your guns and your thugs and your bullshit. Words, Taranto. Words are power."

"What do you have on me, lady? Cut the games and spill it."

Viper said, "Don't tell him." He spoke near her sore ear, his lips moving against it, his breath hot on her throat.

She looked at Lou. "Tell this pig to let go of me."

Lou frowned and finally nodded toward Viper. "You'll have plenty of time to hurt her later on."

She glanced quickly toward Nick. His eyes on her were narrow, and she hoped to God he didn't think this bravado of hers was the real Toni. It wasn't. It was Katrina. Or some messed up combination of the two of them. Or something.

She faced Lou squarely. "I have photos of you passing an envelope to a man named Santos. I have proof that Santos left you and went directly to an airport in Colombia, where he somehow got a job as a mechanic. I have photos of him tinkering with Perez's plane moments before takeoff. I have evidence that a large sum of money was transferred into Santos' bank account the day he arrived in Colombia."

Lou shook his head. "Nothing. It's nothing. Circumstantial, at best."

"I have the envelope."

Lou's brows shot up. "Impossible! Santos said he burned—"

"He put a match to it, dropped it in a trash can. A friend of mine pulled it out and doused the flame. It's charred a little, just around the edges but otherwise, intact." She saw his eyes narrow with skepticism. "Want me to tell you what was inside?"

"You can give it a shot," he said.

"A handwritten note with the name of the little airfield and Perez's flight number and time of departure. Your handwriting, Lou. I checked it against the signature on your driver's license." She shook her head. "Sloppy, sloppy. An expert analyst will use that, you know. There was a nice five-by-seven glossy print of Perez, too. He was wearing a tacky floral-print shirt."

Lou's eyes showed real fear now. "You gave them all of that?"

She shook her head. "You think I'm an idiot? What good would my book be if I gave them all of my surprises? It would all come out in your trial, and all the juice in the book would be old news by the time it hit the shelves. I'd be lucky if it sold a dozen copies."

"But the warrants—"

"I gave them an envelope full of bogus evidence. The photo they have is of my cousin Sam. All the documents are forged, and not very expertly, either. As soon as they realize it, which shouldn't be too far in the future, the warrants will be revoked. They have nothing."

Lou turned, paced the room slowly and came to stand close to her. "How could you know you'd need fake evidence?"

"I'm not new to this game, Taranto. The Feds are always leaning on me to give them what I have before it comes out in the book. I make up phony evidence on a regular basis, just in case. It's my backup plan. If they force the issue, I just give them the fake evidence. That buys me time. My publisher can rush the book to print while they chase their tails trying to verify it. I make a million in royalties, hit the Times list, and *then* hand over the real evidence. This time it paid off."

"So where's the real evidence?"

"I'd be dead in a hurry if I told you that, wouldn't I?"

"Dead, maybe. Not in a hurry. Doesn't matter. You don't have a choice."

"I think I do. A lawyer is holding it for me. I can't even tell you who he is, because I had the arrangements made by my publisher. If anyone makes any attempt to get that envelope—other than me, of course—it goes straight to the DEA. If my publisher doesn't hear from me at least once a day, it goes to them even faster. Now, let's talk, Lou. I stand to make a cool million from the book. You want what I have, you'll have to make me a better offer."

Lou lunged at her, gripped the front of her blouse and pulled her to his face. His rancid breath turned her stomach. "There isn't gonna be any book. You either get me that envelope or you die right here. I guarantee Viper and I can convince you to cooperate."

She tried not to show her fear and revulsion. Her false bravado was draining fast. She felt a tremor go through her heart. "There already *is* a book. I delivered the final draft the day that jerk kidnapped me," she lied. "The deal is, all the evidence goes to the Feds anyway, but not until the book is out."

"Then you can't stop it?" Lou asked, a little of the steel gone from his voice. He stepped away from her, releasing her shirt.

"There's a clause in my contract giving me the right to pull out up to ninety days before publication. That time runs out tomorrow. If you want me to help you out of this, Taranto, you better talk fast. I can make one call at 9:00 a.m. tomorrow that will put the brakes on this entire thing."

Lou cupped his chin in one hand and squeezed. He met Viper's lecherous gaze, and she knew exactly what they were thinking. They'd humor her, offer her whatever she wanted, get the evidence in their filthy hands and then kill her anyway. She didn't care. It would only take a call to the publisher to tell them she'd made the whole thing up anyway. She was betting on its being after hours. They wouldn't be able to confirm her story until morning. She would have bought some time and nothing more.

"How much," Lou finally asked.

She shrugged. "A million-five?"

"Done," he said quickly.

She nodded. "And one more thing. I'll do a lot for that kind of money. But if I'm going to get him killed, I'd just as soon not have to be here to know about it. I do have a few morals. I know you have to do it, but if you want my help you're gonna have to wait until I take my money and leave."

Lou turned a skeptical gaze on her, and she hoped she hadn't blown it by pleading for Nick's life. If Lou knew how much she cared, he'd have the best weapon against her he could've found. He eyed her now, and then Nick.

"You cold, greedy, lying bitch!" Nick's voice was like gravel, so full of venom she almost recoiled. He pulled at his bonds, this time looking as if he'd like to wring her neck with his bare hands. "I'll kill you for this. If I get my hands on you, I'll—"

Viper smacked him in the gut again, knocking enough wind out of him so he couldn't go on. Toni heard the breath rush from his lungs. She turned her back to him, her throat burning, took one step away. She felt drained. All she wanted now was to slink back to her darkened corner and collapse. She'd done all she could, and if Nick couldn't see that, then....

She stopped herself and gave her head a small shake. What was the matter with her? Nick wasn't an idiot. Besides, he knew her better than to believe a word of that line she'd fed Taranto. He knew things about her that she'd only begun to realize about herself. Slowly she turned, and Nick lifted his mistreated face to meet her gaze.

"In the morning, then," Taranto said gruffly. She had to look away from Nick, but not before she'd glimpsed the reassuring glint in his eyes. "You'll make that call. I'll give you the money as soon as the evidence is in my hands. Deal?"

"Deal."

CHAPTER 12

Carl gripped the IV pole with one hand, his heaving stomach with the other. He closed his eyes slowly and waited for the nausea to pass.

"You can barely stand," Joey told him. "You're not gonna to be any help unless you're planning to apprehend Lou Taranto by throwing up on him." Her tone didn't hide the concern in her voice.

"Nausea's normal with concussion. It'll pass." Carl straightened, reached for the closet door and saw his clothes inside. He stretched his arm for the hanger, then paused when his balance deserted him.

Joey reached past him, retrieved his clothes and tossed them on the stiff white sheets on his hospital bed. "'Multiple concussions' was the term I heard them use. Besides, didn't your boss just say they were doing everything that could be done?"

"Yeah, but my boss is in worse shape than I am." Harry had narrowly survived an attempt on his life. Someone had taken a shot at him, probably had mistaken him for Nick, since he'd been driving Nick's car. The bullet grazed his head, and sent him careening off the road and down an embankment. By they time he'd been found, Nick and Toni had already led Taranto and his gang away from Toni's building, giving Toni's sister the chance to get Carl to a hospital. He didn't remember much of that trip.

But no one had heard from Nick or Toni since. Their car had been in an accident. Reports said it was full of bullet holes. But neither of them had been found, and Carl was scared. He sat on the edge of the bed and yanked his trousers on without removing the tie-in-the-back hospital gown he wore. He stood to fasten them, then offered Joey his back.

Sighing, she untied the gown for him. Carl turned again, picked up his shirt and poked his arms into the sleeves. As he buttoned it, he heard her inhale. He looked up fast. Her horrified gaze on his shoulders and chest reminded him the shirt wasn't exactly clean. Looking down, he saw the spattered patterns of dried blood. His lips thinned. He met her gaze again. "Sorry. I didn't think—"

"Taranto has them," she said.

"Can't be sure of that."

"Maybe you can't, but I can."

Lying to her would be useless. She was smart, and a little bit creepy; like she knew things. He figured she'd see right through it. "You're probably right," he admitted. "But don't think that means..." He broke off, searched his foggy brain, and began again. "Taranto thinks he's smart enough to wiggle out of any situation, dodge any charge, no matter how much evidence there is. He won't kill them if he thinks they have information he can use. He'll keep them alive until he gets it from them. Nick knows that, and Toni—she's sharp. She's probably figured it out, too. They can use that knowledge to stall, and in the meantime we'll find out where he's holding them and—"

"I heard your boss—what's his name, the guy who's running the whole operation from his hospital bed down the hall? Harry?" Carl nodded and she went on. "I heard him say they've checked every piece of property Taranto owns and found nothing."

"Every piece we know of," Carl corrected her. "Contrary to popular belief, we don't know everything. Toni already proved that."

A tiny glimmer of hope lit her eyes. "Toni's pretty thorough in her research. She might know of other holdings—"

"If she did, how would I find out?"

Joey dove into the closet. She wasn't reluctant to help him anymore. She retrieved his shoes and socks, his jacket and his gun. "It would be in her computer."

Carl nodded, his mind racing ahead of him as he mindlessly dressed his feet, checked his gun, adjusted the holster. "Okay. Do you have a key to her apartment?" She nodded. "Give it to me and—"

"I'm going with you," she told him.

"No." He straightened too quickly, and the resulting rush of dizziness nearly knocked him down. She came closer to him, gripped his arm until it passed.

"You wouldn't know her passwords. I do. And I'm not telling you. So don't waste time arguing over this. Toni and I share our stubborn streak. Got it from our father."

Carl sighed, pulled on his jacket and turned slightly to close the closet door. It was then he caught a glimpse of his own reflection in the mirror mounted there. He almost jumped. He looked like something from an old Saturday-afternoon horror flick. Dark-colored bruises with angry purple rings at their outermost edges covered most of his face. His nose was bent at an angle near the center. His eyes were still swollen, their lids so blue they looked made-up. He shook his head, closed the door and looked at her again. "I'm surprised you didn't run screaming when you got a look at this." He indicated his face with an open palm beneath his chin.

"I don't scare easily."

She insisted on driving—and when he saw what, he was even more nervous. Toni Rio's sister got around by means of a sweet cherry red Harley. "How the hell did you get me to the hospital on that?"

"I only got you around the corner on it. Then I called an ambulance. You don't remember?"

"No. Thank God." He hopped on and within thirty minutes he was standing behind her in the office of Toni's apartment. Joey Bradshaw sat in a padded swivel chair, punching buttons on her sister's keyboard. "I'm surprised the cops didn't take this."

"Oh, they will, trust me. They haven't processed the apartment yet. Everyone's out looking for Taranto and Nick." There was crime scene tape across the front of the door, but no one stood guard. Toni's evidence was all in police custody already, thanks so her sister. No one was overly concerned about the apartment.

"And Toni," she added.

In a moment the words "Holdings: Real Estate" appeared on the screen. Joey scrolled slowly down the list, and Carl's eyes sped over every line, his impatience nearing an all-time high. Then he saw what he was looking for.

"There! Number eighteen, that's one I've never heard of. I don't think we knew about that one."

Joey clicked on the listing. "Farmhouse," the screen told them. "Rural Chenango County—Upstate N.Y." Carl read that Taranto had purchased the property for back taxes, using his cousin's name on the deed. Toni's notes said she had suspected the place was a dispatch point for drugs being shipped to Syracuse, Binghamton and other surrounding cities. The house itself, she'd noted, was in a state of chronic disrepair, but ideal for Lou's purposes, being completely surrounded by state forest.

Carl shook his head, a sickening feeling in his stomach that hadn't been caused by his concussions this time. "How do we find this place?"

"It's just over an hour from where I live. I know the area." Joey yanked out her cell phone, opened the map feature and tapped in the address. "It's a four-hour drive from here."

"Who said anything about driving?"

It was several moments before Nick could speak again. The last blow to the midsection had struck a rib on the way in. He couldn't draw a breath. He forcibly clung to consciousness despite the pain that washed over him like a tidal wave and the dizziness it brought with it. He had to stay lucid. At least until he could be sure Toni knew why he'd said what he had. When she'd asked that he not be killed right way, Taranto got suspicious. Nick knew him well enough to recognize the look. He had to do something to convince Lou that there was nothing between them.

Taranto and Viper left the room, and he heard locks being slid home. A second later Toni was behind him, deftly untying his hands. Circling to the front of him, she dropped to her knees and loosened the ropes that held his ankles. She stayed there a minute, not looking up.

Then she took a deep breath and said, "I hope I'm right about how well you know me, Nick."

He rubbed his wrists roughly, then put both hands on her shoulders. "You put on one hell of an act, Toni. And you'd better damn well know by now when I'm doing the same. Call it a supporting role."

Her head rose slowly, her eyes scanning his face. "You knew what I was doing?"

"Almost as soon as you did. It never entered my

mind to believe a word of it." He closed his arms around her, but she stiffened and held herself away.

"You're hurt pretty badly, Nick." Her eyes danced back and forth as she studied his face. "I wanted to club that bastard with something...I almost jumped on him without anything but my hands to use as weapons."

"I believe you." He smiled to show her he was okay, but she touched his face gently with her palm, and her eyes got damp again. "I'm fine, I swear to God. It probably looks worse than it is." Seeing the fear in her eyes was more than he could handle right then, so he tried to change the subject. "You were good with Taranto, Toni. You pinpointed his weakness and you nailed him with it. He'd do anything to save his organization."

She shook her head, getting to her feet. "He'll be angrier than ever when he finds out I was lying."

Nick rose, as well, glancing around the musty room. "You bought us some time. Now all we need to do is find a way out of here. It's a basement...a cellar. This is just a house, and not a new one by the looks. I wonder where the hell we are?" He walked as he spoke, examining the rotted wood, the toppled water tank, the broken wooden crate. He knelt beside it and pawed through the dust-covered bottom to identify the shapes there. He found bent nails, a broken screwdriver and some wire. He tucked the screwdriver into his rear pocket and got upright again, glancing upward at the cobweb-coated ceiling.

"Not a heating duct or a register in the place," he

muttered.

"I don't think anyone's been here in a while," Toni observed.

"You're right. He had to bring us somewhere isolated. With warrants out on him, he couldn't risk staying around the city, much less any of his known hangouts. He can't have had time to round up much help, either. I imagine most of his thugs scattered once the feds served the search warrants on Taranto's businesses."

He stared at the door, frustration rising within him. "If we could get through the damn door, we might have a chance." He paced the room. "What if I make some racket, get whoever's guarding the door to open it up?" He was thinking aloud, the plan coming together in his mind as he voiced it. "I could jump the guy when he comes in. You could run out, close the door so he couldn't yell or come after you."

She closed her eyes slowly and shook her head. "No." When she opened her eyes again, the look in them was intense. She held his gaze forcefully. "Listen to me for once, Nick. I will not leave you." He frowned, searching her face, and she caught his face between her cool palms and held his eyes with hers. "I mean it. I won't."

He sensed she wanted him to read more into her words than what she'd said, and the idea awed him. Could she be trying to tell him that—

No. In his entire life, no one had ever cared enough about him to stay for the long haul. How likely was it that a woman like Toni Rio, the smartest, sexiest, bravest woman he'd ever met, would be the first? He shook his head at the impossibility of it. Still, some small part of him wondered. She hadn't left him yet, though remaining with him had put her at risk. She hadn't left him, even when he'd tried to make her go.

"Toni, this might be your last chance. I'm offering you a way out. I don't see any other options."

"He'd kill you," she said softly. "He'd have no reason not to."

"If you stay, he'll kill us both," he told her.

She sighed, looked at the floor. "You really think I could just walk away from you, Nick? After all of this? I can't, you know. I couldn't if I wanted to. I won't. Even..." She drew a steadying breath and brought her gaze up to his. "Even when it's over."

He couldn't believe what he saw in her eyes. It hit him harder than Viper had, rendering him speechless. He opened his mouth, and only air came out.

The sound of a key turning in the lock startled him. Toni shoved him away, both hands flat on his chest. He knew she intended for him to sit down, as if he were still bound. He didn't, though. He couldn't take his eyes off her face. He couldn't stop his heart from pounding. This was not the time or the place, but he thought she might trying to tell him she loved him.

The door opened, and two men he hadn't seen before stepped through it. Both held guns, and both barrels were trained on Nick.

"You!" The fifty-something thug with the crew

cut and brown teeth waggled his gun barrel toward Toni. "Come with us."

"She's not going anywhere," Nick said softly.

"What's a matter, Manelli? You want to keep her all to yourself, is that it?"

The one beside Brown Teeth shifted his stance. He was younger, with a pocked face and body like a bean pole. "I don't know about this," he muttered. "Lou said not to touch her until he got what he wanted from her."

"There won't be anything left to touch when he's got what he wants from her, kid. You ever seen what Lou does to broads that fuck him over?" He shook his head and moved closer to Toni. His gaze moved down her body slowly, and Nick clenched his teeth. "I won't hurt you, babe. I know how to handle a woman. You might even like me." He licked his lips. "You don't come along like a good girl, though, and I'll have to put a bullet in Nicky. See, Lou would kill me if I hurt you. But I have permission to shoot *him* if he gives me a reason."

Nick saw Toni's eyes harden. It amazed him once again, the backbone she had. He knew at that moment that all his resolve hadn't amounted to a damn thing. He'd been in love with her all along.

"That's right, sweet thing. I can see you realize you got no choice. You give me trouble, you get to watch him die and then you do what I tell you anyway, right? So why get Nicky blown away for nothing? You just come with me and you keep what I said in mind while we're in the other room." He glanced at the younger one. "I think she's gonna be real willing to accommodate us, Ray. I think she'll do anything we tell her to. Won't you, babe?"

She didn't answer until the younger one lifted the muzzle of his gun to Nick's temple. Nick's eyes were on Toni as she stiffened her spine. "I'll come with you."

"The hell you will," Nick said.

"They won't kill me, Nick."

"They won't touch you."

He heard her stifle a sob. She swallowed. "I don't want to lose you like this," she rasped. "Let it go. It won't be me, I swear to you. They'll be touching an empty shell—"

"Enough! Anybody'd think you had a choice about it." Brown Teeth grabbed Toni's upper arm. "Come on, baby, I been waitin' for this." He yanked her toward the door.

The younger one pressed the barrel harder to Nick's temple, but Nick's eyes were on Toni. Her gaze sent him a silent message, begging him not to do anything. Aloud she whispered again, "It won't be me, Nick."

"You're damn right it won't," he growled. In one swift move, he'd pulled the broken screwdriver from his pocket and jammed it into the skinny man, just below the rib cage, angling upward and thrusting it clear to the handle. His gun thudded to the floor. Brown Teeth turned at the sound, saw his partner drop to his knees, mouth agape. He released his hold on Toni and leveled his gun at Nick. Toni slammed her fists down on his forearms. The gun roared, deafening in the small room, but the bullet only embedded itself in the packed dirt of the floor. Nick used the split second Toni had bought him to lunge for the gun at his feet. He had it in his hand when Brown Teeth backhanded Toni, slamming her into the cinder-block wall. Nick pulled the trigger, sending another earsplitting boom into the confined space. The man staggered backward three steps, then folded in on himself, ending in a heap on the floor.

Nick reached down, twisted the gun from his limp grasp and straightened again. Toni stood near the doorway, her gaze on the bleeding skinny one with the screwdriver handle protruding from his belly. He was unconscious but still alive. Nick stepped over Brown Teeth, pressed the gun into Toni's hand, gripped her chin, forced her to look at him. "We're getting out of here."

She nodded, and they headed out through the small doorway, both knowing those gunshots must've been heard upstairs.

They entered the main part of an ancient, crumbling cellar. He felt her body tremble as he urged her through. Already he heard footsteps above. Nick glanced to the left and saw the rickety stairs that led upward, presumably to the house. To the right was another, less steep, set, with an angular hatch like door that laid almost flat at the top that would lead outside. There were more footsteps from above, and raised voices. He put his arm around her shoulders, mounted the first step and heard the door at the top of the other set of stairs creak open. If this exit was locked—

He shoved at the hatch, and it swung open, hitting the ground hard. They sped out into the warm, fresh night air and pitch dark. His stride lengthened. "Run, Toni!" She did, clutching his hand tightly, and in seconds bullets flew after them.

They were not in New York City anymore. They crossed a dewy, overgrown lawn with weeds that reached above his knees. At its edge, a dirt road twisted away into blackness. Nick glanced back. He saw only a tall, sagging house silhouetted by the half moon—and muzzle flashes like murderous eyes. He pulled her with him again, crossing the dirt track and heading for the thick woods opposite. They were at the edge of the tree line when he heard her suck in her breath and felt her hand clutch his tighter.

Fear hit him between the eyes. He paused just beyond the trees. "Toni?"

She didn't stop when he did. "Nothing—twisted my ankle. Come on!" She tugged at his hand.

He could hear their pursuers coming closer. They ran, heading deeper into the forest. The pain of his broken rib screamed angrily.

They approached a sharp rise and took it at a brutal pace. Nick began to worry. Just where the hell were they? How far could this forest go on? Towering spruce trees surrounded them, angling skyward even on this steep hillside. The ground underfoot gave softly with their steps, making little sound. They topped the rise and started down the opposite side. A fallen tree caught his eye, and Nick noticed the cavelike space formed by the awkwardly bent boughs and the steep incline. He pulled Toni to it, and they ducked inside. She sat down, and Nick glanced through the opening, seeing no one at the moment.

"How big can these damn woods be?"

She was breathing hard. Too hard. "Thousands of acres," she said. "It's state forest."

He turned, frowning, and crouched beside her. Even in the darkness he could see the deep stain on her shirt. Her sleeve was soaked, dripping. "You're hit! Why didn't you say something?" He forgot his own pain, that of his unhealed thigh and even of the broken rib, as he unbuttoned the blouse quickly, shoved it down over her shoulders and yanked it from her hands. She winced when the material pulled away from the wound in her shoulder. Blood pulsed from a small hole. Nick swore. The exertion of running had only increased the bleeding. He tore the clean sleeve off her blouse and twisted it around her, under her arm and over her shoulder, then tied it tight.

He watched for a moment, unsure whether he'd stopped the blood flow or just slowed it. Damn the darkness. How much blood had she lost already? Angrily he tore the bloody sleeve off and helped her slip her arms back into the now-sleeveless blouse. He buttoned it with badly shaking hands.

When he finished, he glanced up at her face. She leaned back against the sticky trunk, her eyes closed.

"Toni? Talk to me. Does it hurt much?"

"It's okay. I'm just resting." She opened her eyes, but it seemed to be an effort. Her voice was weak. "I remember now—it's some rural county. I forget the name. Upstate."

He slipped his hand to the back of her head and pulled her forward until she rested on his shoulder. "You'll be okay." Was he comforting her or himself? "You'll be okay, Toni. I'll get you out of this, I swear I will." He couldn't lose her. He couldn't. He held her tighter.

She lifted her head. "We should go...farther. They'll come after us."

Nick studied her eyes, silently begging her not to leave him this way. "Just rest. It's dark. They'd have to trip over us to find us here." He pulled her head back down gently. "Just rest."

"I don't want to rest." She remained relaxed against him despite her words. "I have to tell you... not to feel guilty. None..." She drew a deep breath and seemed to steady herself. "None of this was your fault."

"Shh." He stroked her hair. God, how he loved her hair. "You can ease my conscience when you're feeling better."

"But...what if I don't—"

"Don't even say it, lady. You aren't getting away from me that easy."

He felt her sigh. "You're right." Her voice was barely a whisper now. "I told you I wouldn't leave you, Nick. I meant it. You have to know that. I meant it." She lifted her head again, and it seemed to take an incredible effort. She gazed into his eyes. "I know it'll be hard for you to believe me. Everyone you ever loved walked out on you. You don't trust anyone. But I won't walk out, Nick. Not unless you ask me to. Maybe not even then." Her eyes closed slowly and popped wide again as if she'd forced them. "I love you, Nick Manelli."

He felt as if he'd been struck by lightning. "You—you're delirious."

"I love you." Her head fell to his shoulder as if she could no longer hold it up.

Nick caught her face in his hands and gently lifted her, but her eyes remained closed, thick lashes resting on her cheeks, tears glistening in the single shaft of moonlight that made its way between the pine boughs. He kissed her, but her lips were slack and unresponsive. He closed his arms around her and rocked her slowly as a burning dampness gathered in his eyes. "Hold on, Toni. You said you wouldn't go and I'm holding you to it."

She loved him. My God, it was not possible. No one had ever uttered those three words to Nick before—not even his own mother. Yet Toni had. She said she loved him, and he believed her.

She shivered in his arms. She needed help; he knew that. She'd lost a lot of blood, running full tilt the way she had while her magnificent heart pumped more and more blood out of her body. He lowered her gently, then moved out of the sheltering boughs and paused, listening. He heard Taranto's men moving, but in the wrong direction.

Apparently they'd passed by and were still heading deeper into the woods. Nick bent and lifted Toni carefully into his arms. He'd take her back the way they'd come. There must be a vehicle, a phone, something.

He'd carried her nearly all the way back. The dirt road should be just beyond his range of vision now. She hadn't stirred in all that time. A sense of dread had settled over him. To lose her now would kill him. He drew closer to the road, able to see its shape. He was about to step through the last line of trees when he heard the choppers. They approached fast, and in seconds hovered over him. Spotlights swept through the trees over the road and seemed to settle on a subject. An artificially amplified voice filled the air, all but drowned out by the pounding of the chopper blades, but audible and mad as hell. "We are federal officers. Stand where you are and throw your weapons to the ground."

There was sudden movement from the road, and a burst of gunfire. Nick lowered Toni to the ground and lifted his weapon just as Lou Taranto lunged through the trees directly in front of him. Nick heard one of the choppers touch down. Lou lifted his gun muzzle.

"Forget it, Lou," Nick said, his voice level. "You're going down this time. It's over."

Taranto's gun wavered. "Like my own son, Nicky." His body shook now, as well as his hand. "I treated you like my own son. You're right, it's over. But not just for me." The change in his grip on the revolver was minuscule but enough. Nick pulled the trigger three times in quick succession, and each time Lou's fat body jerked as if electrocuted. He went down then and lay still on the ground.

Nick looked at him for a long moment. He'd been waiting for this from the time he was sixteen years old, and now that it had come, it was nothing. It meant nothing. All that mattered was Toni. He turned and bent low to lift her into his arms again.

"Not yet, Manelli."

Viper's voice came from just behind him, and Nick's blood went cold. He'd lowered his weapon too soon. He stiffened, not even breathing, and lifted his gun, ready to spin and fire, and knowing he couldn't move fast enough.

The sudden crack that split the air behind him jolted him, but Nick felt no bullet. He whirled, ready to fire, not believing Viper had missed. But Viper lay dead on the ground. Nick looked past the hit man to see Carl's garishly bruised face. He stood with one hand braced against a tree trunk and gave Nick a lopsided grin.

"How many times are you gonna make me save that overdeveloped butt of yours, pal? I'm getting kinda sick of it."

"By my count, that makes us about even, Salducci." Nick turned, holstering his gun, and bent over Toni again. He picked her up and walked toward the road.

"She okay?"

"She has to be," Nick said. "I'm on a roll."

He stepped out of the trees onto the road and saw cops everywhere and several of Taranto's men being handcuffed. Toni's sister, Joey, ran toward him, shaking an officer's restraining hands off her as if they were nothing. She stopped in front of Nick, her hand smoothing Toni's hair.

"Oh, God..."

"She's only unconscious," Nick said gently. "She's going to be all right."

She nodded brusquely, stepped to one side, keeping her hand on her sister's face and walking along with him toward the nearest chopper. "Yeah. Yeah, she will." There was relief in her voice, then she looked up at him. "She looks better than you do, I can tell you that much."

Nick heard the slight waver underlying the gusto of her words. He saw her lower lip tremble and he spotted droplets forming on her lashes. What was it with these women and their false bravado, anyway?

CHAPTER 13

When Nick saw Joey's gaze jump just before she got to her feet, he knew the surgeon had finally come out of the O.R. of the tiny Community Memorial Hospital in the town of Hamilton. It was a good hospital. Nick had checked. And the guy was a good surgeon. He'd checked on that, too. He'd had little else to do in the four hours since they'd rushed Toni through the double doors with the signs proclaiming Absolutely No Admittance Beyond This Point. He got his rib cage wrapped, his lacerations stitched, his thigh re-bandaged, then he sat in anguish trying not to think of Toni as he'd last seen her; pale and limp and so damn weak.

She'd told him she loved him. He still wasn't over the shock of it. She'd meant it, too; it showed in her eyes. She loved him. It was a miracle—the only one he'd had in his life. Maybe you were only entitled to one. He'd damn well like another one. He wanted her to be all right. He couldn't lose her now.

"Miss Bradshaw, Mr. Manelli?"

He snapped to attention. The surgeon stood in front of him. Nick didn't know when he'd stood up. He looked at the man's blue pouffy paper hat and at the mask he'd tugged down so it hung around his neck. He couldn't seem to meet the man's eyes. His fear of seeing the worst there kept his gaze darting around the waiting room. The smell began to get to him. He felt it must have permeated his body by now. He felt as if he'd still smell it even if he burned his clothes and took ten scalding showers. He felt—

"Thank God," Joey whispered. She turned to Nick, hugged his neck, wobbled very slightly, and Nick put his arms around her shoulders to steady her. "She's okay, Nick. She's gonna be okay."

Nick could've sworn every muscle in his body melted in relief. "When can I—can we—see her?" he managed.

"She's in recovery," the doctor said. "She lost a lot of blood, won't wake for several hours. I'd advise you to get some rest, something to eat. Someone will let you know the minute she starts to come around."

"She's going to be okay," Nick muttered, almost in disbelief as the doctor strode away from them.

Joey straightened and looked up at him. "Yeah, but are you?"

He shook his head. "Two miracles in one day. It's hard to swallow." She was all right. She loved him and she was all right. Suddenly, he grinned, feeling like a small boy on Christmas morning. "I've never been better!" He grabbed Toni's sister and hugged her hard enough to force the air from her lungs. "I've gotta go out, but I won't be long. Text me the second you hear anything."

He walked on air through the corridors, and managed to commandeer a local cop's car for his purposes. Then he drove away from the neat, low brick building, through the college town and into the rural countryside. He left the windows down so that wonderful fresh-cut-grass fragrance could waft over him, and he tried to imagine what on earth he'd done to deserve to be loved by a woman like Toni.

As he drove, the houses grew farther apart. He passed green meadows, fenced fields and herds of lazy fat cows. He drove by a huge rambling Victorian house and he smiled, remembering the way Toni had confided her secret dreams to him, afraid he'd think they were silly.

He didn't. He couldn't for the life of him imagine a better way to spend his life than with Toni in some big old house. They'd fix it up together, and she'd have an office with lots of light. She could work on those warm, uplifting books she wanted to write. He'd join the local P.D. When he came home at night, she'd be there. She wouldn't walk out. She loved him.

He smiled, suddenly knowing exactly what he wanted to get for her. The doctor had said several hours. Would he have time to find what he needed?

The afternoon sun slanted in through a window and heated Toni's face and eyelids. The smells around her were clean and familiar. Hospital smells, she realized. Her throat hurt. It felt dry and as if something had scraped it raw. There was no pain in her shoulder. Somehow she thought there should be.

She opened her eyes. Nick sat beside the bed in a chair. He held her hand tightly, she realized. He looked better than he had. His cheek was still swollen and purple, but not as bad as it had been. The blood had all been washed away from his bruised face.

He looked relieved when she met his eyes, but nervous, too. "Hey, sleepyhead. Feel up to a five-mile run?"

She smiled at him and her heart swelled when she thought of how much she loved him. She'd told him so, hadn't she? When they'd been in the forest, and she'd thought she might die, she'd decided to tell him exactly how she felt, in case she never had another chance. Maybe that was why he seemed nervous. She'd scared him with the intensity of her feelings.

He smiled back at her. "You don't know how good it is to see that smile of yours, Toni." He leaned close and kissed her with exquisite tenderness. When he straightened, he studied her face as if he was drinking it in.

She lifted one hand—the only one she seemed able to move—and ran it through her hair. "I'm a mess," she said.

"You're gorgeous."

"My hair—"

"You'd be gorgeous bald, lady."

That remark elicited a giggle, but Nick wasn't smiling. His face was serious. "You remember what happened?"

Her smile faded. She nodded and glanced down at her arm. Her shoulder was heavily bandaged, her arm in a sling. "I was shot."

"The arm will be fine, Toni. No complications. A few weeks and you'll be as good as new."

She frowned. "Was my sister there? Where is she? Is she okay?"

He nodded. "She fell asleep in the other chair, woke up looking like she'd seen a ghost, and said she had to go. Something about her other sister being in trouble."

She lifted her brows. "Caroline. Joey's real sister. Well, the one she was raised with, anyway. She's sweet, even if she doesn't like me very much. I think I'm a reminder that their sainted mother had an affair. But then, so is Joey." She blinked slowly. "I hope she's all right."

He frowned. "You have any reason to think she's not?"

"Joey...she knows things sometimes. Sees things. In her mind." She sighed. "I'll call her later, find out what's up." The frown left her brows and she gazed at his face. "How are you, Nick? Are you okay?"

"Physically, yeah. The rest...kind of depends on you." He cleared his throat, lowered his eyes. "Do—um—you remember what you told me out there in the woods?"

She drew a deep breath. "I didn't mean to make you uncomfortable. I was afraid I wouldn't make it. I wanted you to know—"

"Then you meant it?"

He seemed so uncertain all of a sudden, and kind of vulnerable. Frowning, she looked into his eyes. "I'm in love with you, Nick. Maybe I shouldn't have said it so soon, but I'm not going to take it back now."

"I'm glad you said it." He looked at her, and for a moment she thought there was a bit more moisture in his eyes than usual. "No one's ever said it to me before."

"Then you don't mind?" He shook his head. Toni sighed. "I love you," she told him. "I love you enough to make up for all the people who didn't. More than enough...if you'll let me."

He pressed his palms gently to either side of her face and kissed her again. "I love you so much I would have died if I had lost you." He carefully gathered her to him and kissed her even more deeply, letting his feelings rush over her and through her. She felt the lack of reservation and restraint and she gloried in it.

When he eased her down onto her pillows, she felt caught in a whirlwind. "I'm not sure what this means. Where do we go from here?"

"Anywhere we want, that's the icing on the cake. Toni, do you realize how well our dreams mesh? Your big rural house, my small-town beat...and...." He bent low and scooped something from the floor.

"And this," he whispered.

She frowned as he set a small basket in her lap, then lifted the lid and peered inside. A furry white head popped out and a tiny tongue bathed her in puppy kisses. Her breath caught in her throat, and the tears she'd been holding back spilled over. She reached her good hand inside and pulled the tiny gray-and-white fur ball out, held him close to her, and the puppy nuzzled her neck. "He's a sheepdog! I can't believe you did this, Nick."

"I'm calling him Ralph," he told her. "If that's okay with you."

"It's more than okay with me. It's perfect. You're perfect."

"I wasn't," he said. "I was missing a piece before. But then I found you. I love you, Toni Rio. I'm gonna love you for a long, long time."

"I'm counting on it," she whispered.

–THE END–

Don't miss the rest of the
SHATTERED SISTERS SERIES.

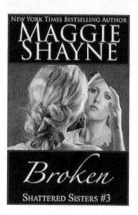

Continue Reading for an excerpt from
FORGOTTEN.

FORGOTTEN

He was the key.

Joey Bradshaw shifted in the hard little chair and studied him. It was the first time she'd seen him... with her eyes. Everything was the same, though. The square, cruel jawline, the thick, dark lashes that tried to soften its effect, the tiny, crescent-shaped scar amid the curling black hairs at his wrist. His hair seemed blue black against the stiff, white linens. The only difference was that, at the moment, he was breathing. Even his scent was exactly as she'd imagined it. A blend of blatant male virility and some spicy shaving cream. Such a potent mix was a pleasant distraction from the disinfectant aroma of the hospital.

She'd left her half sister Toni in a hospital not far from this one only a few weeks ago. Toni was fine. All wrapped up in testifying against a drug kingpin, promoting her brand new true crime book, and house hunting with the man who'd won her heart and got her a puppy instead of an engagement ring.

Joey's other sister, Caroline, might not be so fine. And that was why Joey was here.

The handsome man's eyes opened, blinked into focus and narrowed as he studied her. Beyond his curious expression she saw nothing. They were empty, those deep brown eyes. Vacant, just as the doctors had warned her they would be. It was cruel, what she had to do to him. It might not even work. But what choice did she have, really? She'd foreseen her sister Caroline's murder. It was going to happen right after the murder of the man in the bed.

"Do I know you?" He sat up slightly as he spoke and the sheet slipped down to his waist. He wore no hospital gown. The sight of his tanned skin, stretched taut over a broad chest sent a little shiver of pure appreciation up her spine. In answer to his question, she nodded.

He shook his head, frustration showing in the way his gaze intensified. "Bad enough I couldn't remember my own name. I can't believe any blow to the head would make me forget *you*, lady, whoever you are."

Heat crept up her neck and yet another round of doubt came with it, She wasn't sure if his lighthearted flirting would make this easier or harder. Especially since the attraction was mutual. She'd prepared herself for the sexual magnetism that drew her to him. She'd sensed it before she'd ever come here— and decided she could handle it. But if it was a two-way street, traveling it might get damned complicated.

For a moment she seriously considered getting out of her chair, walking out the door and never turning back. She'd spent too much time in hospitals lately. She'd almost lost one sister to the mob. Now another sister was in the sites of a serial killer.

No rest for the gifted, she supposed.

Then she glanced at his chest again, and in a flash that left her dizzy, she saw it bloody; pale skin between splashes of crimson. She felt the stillness of once-powerful lungs, and the deadening silence of a magnificent heart.

"Hey. Are you okay?"

Joey forced her white-knuckled grip on the chair arms to ease and dragged her gaze from his chest, back up to his milk-chocolate eyes. Numbly she nodded. She shifted in the chair, leather creaking against vinyl.

"You gonna tell me who you are, or am I supposed to guess?"

"You'd never guess in a million years," she said softly to the man she'd never met until today. "I'm your wife."

"My...*what?*"

"Your wife."

He shook his head slowly and she could feel how badly it ached. A white bandage at the back of his skull stood like a banner of surrender amid his soft, sooty hair. The car accident that had put him here had caused no other injury. Only that one blow to the head, and the resulting memory loss. For Joey's purposes, it was the perfect opportunity to intervene in a deadly situation.

"My wife." He closed his eyes briefly, then opened them again, studying her with poorly disguised skepticism.

"You don't believe me."

He shrugged, eyes narrow, almost mocking. What had happened to the emptiness? Her mind was wide open. The problem was, she had no control over what she "picked up," and what she didn't. The images, the feelings, were random. God knew there were some things she'd rather not feel at all. Sickening, horrible things.

"I don't believe much of anything until I see proof," he told her. "That's just the way I am."

She frowned. "And how do you know *what* way you are?"

The sardonic smile died and the clouds returned to his eyes. "I don't know. That just came out." He shook his head slowly.

Joey felt a rush of sympathy for him, followed quickly by a rush of guilt. Her presence here wouldn't make things any easier. "It must be pretty lousy, forgetting your entire life." Worse yet, with what she was doing to him.

He searched her face. "I've talked to the people I work with—"

"At the *Chronicle,*" she inserted, just to show him she knew.

He nodded, his gaze intensifying, never wavering from hers. "They filled in a lot of the blanks for me. But no one mentioned a wife. How do you explain that?"

She wasn't unprepared. She'd known which bases would need covering, and she'd covered them. He had no family, or none she'd been able to trace. There would be no doubting in-laws to contend with. She called to mind the lines she'd rehearsed for this moment and cleared her throat. "Did they tell you about your weekend in Vegas?"

He nodded, his face wary. "I went there to follow up a lead on...a story."

"The Syracuse Slasher." His eyes widened, but he hid his surprise quickly. "Your lead was a dead end. But the trip wasn't entirely wasted." She reached down to the backpack on the floor beside her and pulled out the rolled, ribboned document. The scent of fresh ink worried her, but she doubted he'd notice that. She handed it to him, kept talking as he unrolled it. "When you asked me to go along, I had no idea what you were planning, Ash."

He frowned over the marriage certificate that proclaimed Ashville Allan Coye and Josephine Belinda Bradshaw were husband and wife. For what she'd paid for the thing, he'd better not find a single flaw.

Finally he shook his head. "So I have a wife. It's so odd. It's like I've never seen you before in my life. I hope that doesn't hurt your feelings too badly."

"I knew what to expect." She swallowed, failing to remove the hard lump in her throat

"So we were just married on Saturday?" he asked. "And no one else knew about it?"

"That's right. We arrived back on Sunday night. I went to my house and you went back to your apartment...to pack a few things, you said. When you didn't come back, I didn't know what to think."

"And now that you know?"

She drew a bracing breath and steadied her jangling nerves. It was necessary, she reminded herself. If she let him out of her sight for a minute, it could mean disaster. And this was the only way. She couldn't very well go to the police. They'd laugh her right out of the building. They'd never believe her. Very few people ever had. It was sickeningly ironic that she could get people to accept lies more easily than the truth. The super at the building where Ash lived, for example. He'd bought this same story, hook, line and sinker, and unlocked the apartment for her. If she'd told him the truth, he'd have dialed 911 to report a woman having an obvious psychotic break.

Except with her dad. The one who'd raise her, not the one who'd sired her, He'd never doubted her gift. He'd never accused her of having an overactive imagination. But he was nothing to her now. Less than nothing.

"Well?" Ash prompted, reminding her he'd asked a question.

She straightened her spine, met his velvety brown gaze. "I'm hoping we can pick up where we left off." She let her eyes search his face, tried to put longing into her expression. It was easier than it ought to be. "That is...if you still want to."

Ash felt his eyebrows arch. So she wanted to play house with him. Well, that would require some serious consideration. He studied her again. Her hair was a mixture of honey gold and strawberry blond. It was wild and long. His gaze lingered on her exotically slanted, emerald green eyes and the black velvet forest surrounding them. She was small, no more than five feet tall, and she had incredible legs. No contour was hidden beneath the skintight leather pants she wore. The rest of her shape was concealed by her matching jacket. She smelled like fresh air and leather, and she looked at him like she was trying to see right through him.

"Can we do that, Ash? Pick up where we left off?"

He licked his lips. "I'm thinking." Who the hell *was* she, anyway? What was her game?

She rose, scooping her backpack from the floor and dropping it on the chair. Then, turning her back to him, she bent over it. He heard the rasp of the zipper, watched her rummage around in the bag. Watching the subtle movements of her black-leather-encased, perfectly round backside, he felt himself inclined to go along with her scheme, whatever it was.

When she turned, she held a pair of jeans—*his jeans*—and a pale gray button-down dress shirt. Holy shit, she'd been in his apartment.

"These are for when you're released." She opened

the narrow closet opposite the bed and busied herself hanging the clothes. She'd brought socks, too, underwear, his cross trainers. He noticed that her hands trembled just slightly as she stowed each item in the closet. "I wasn't sure what kind of shape your other clothes were in, after the accident."

He just watched her. She was obviously nervous, seemingly making things up as she went along. She couldn't seem to hold his gaze or sit still or stop filling the tense silence. "Is there anything else I can bring you? Magazines or books or—"

"No." He was baffled. "Look, um..." He glanced down at the marriage certificate in his hand. "Josephine—" She grimaced and her nose wrinkled. Damn. When she wasn't outrageously sexy, she was unbearably cute.

"It's Joey, and I'll only forgive that mistake once, amnesia or no amnesia."

He couldn't help but smile as he tapped the paper in his hand. "That's not what it says here. Josephine Belinda Bradshaw."

"Well, regardless of what it says there, my name is Joey." Her lashes lowered over those impossibly green eyes and she added, "Joey Coye."

He shook his head. He'd have to resist the cries of his body that were telling him to go along with her scam, whatever it was, just in case she planned to let him exercise a few husbandly prerogatives. He reminded himself that women like her were not his type. And that this was a serious game she was playing. She was up to something.

"Okay. Joey, then. Do you mind me asking how you got into my apartment?"

Her eyes focused on his, filled with enough innocence to fool the devil himself. "You gave me a key, Ash."

"Oh."

The investigative reporter inside jumped with questions. His libido was making noises of surrender. Loud noises. But the still-small voice of self-preservation squeaked its dissent.

Because, after all, the accident had been no accident. Someone was trying very hard to kill him.

Then again, forewarned was forearmed, right? And what better way to find out what she was up to than to play this out? She certainly looked harmless enough.

"Ash? Is anything wrong?"

He sighed. "No. As a matter of fact, you couldn't have come at a better time. They're springing me today."

Her eyes doubled in size at that instant. "T-today?"

"Yeah. Got the news ten minutes before you got here. So if you'll hand me those clothes, I'll be ready to leave by the time they bring in my discharge papers."

"Leave?"

"You *are* taking me home, aren't you?" He was enjoying her panic, but he was careful not to show it. He kept his expression blank, trusting.

"Home? I don't—"

"No." He stopped her before she could say

anything else. Eyes downcast, he bit his lower lip to keep from grinning. "It's okay, I understand. I thought when you said you wanted to pick up where we left off..." He swallowed an imaginary lump. "It's all right. What kind of a husband would I be, like this?"

He'd called her bluff. He'd watched her squirm, and now he was giving her a way out. Obviously whatever scam she was pulling wasn't meant to extend beyond this hospital room. He could wait until later to do a background check on her, figure out what this fiasco had been all about.

But wait a minute. Oh, hell no! She marched to that closet, gathered up his clothes, brought them to the bed, then perched on the mattress and gripped his shoulders. Her eyes stabbed into his with unmistakable sincerity and some kind of raw power.

No eyes had ever been that green. She had to be wearing tinted contacts. Didn't she?

"Don't ever let me hear you talk that way again," she told him. "I was just taken by surprise. I didn't realize they'd let you go so soon with a head injury this serious. I figured..." She shook her head fast and her crazy curls swung back and forth over her face. "Of course I'm taking you home. I wouldn't have it any other way."

He frowned, wondering how she managed to seem so genuine when she was lying though her teeth. Damn, she was good. "Are you sure?"

Her shoulders squared and her spine stiffened. Determination lit her eyes. "Get dressed, Ash. I'll go and see about getting your release forms and we'll get out of here."

He nodded and watched the sway of her hips, as mesmerizing as a hypnotist's pocket watch, as she turned and left. When the door closed, he shook himself, got out of the bed, went to the door and cracked it, just to be sure she wasn't standing outside. Then he grabbed his phone.

When he heard his editor's voice on the line, he didn't waste time with preamble. "There's a drop-dead gorgeous woman here claiming to be my wife, Rad. She wants to take me home. I'm going."

Radley Ketchum chortled. "You? Married? Ash, maybe they'd better x-ray your head one more time, huh? What's going on?"

"I'm serious." Ash darted a glance toward the door and rushed on. "She has a certificate that says I married her in Vegas on Saturday."

"And she expects you to buy it? You? The most dedicated bachelor in the state of New York?"

"Well, she probably figures I don't know that, don't you think?"

Rad was silent for a long moment. "Look, you better not go with her. This whole deal was supposed to keep you alive, not get you killed."

He thought about the look in Joey Bradshaw's eyes when he'd pretended emotional agony. "I don't think it's her."

"Oh, no? What makes you so sure?"

Ash shook his head. "I don't know. Gut feeling, maybe."

"Does she smoke?"

"How the hell do I know if she smokes? Look, I'll let you know where I am when I get there, okay?"

"She lights up a cigarette, my friend, you get the hell out. You have any urge to stick around, you just think about those butts with the coral-frost lipstick stains on them that the cops found at the scenes of all three murders."

"Yeah. Don't worry, I'm not suicidal."

"One more thing. Get her address on record somewhere before you leave the hospital, just in case you can't call with it later. Phone number, too. Give me her name right now and I'll see what I can find out about her."

"Her name, she says, is Mrs. Ashville Coye."

"Very funny."

"The marriage certificate reads Josephine Belinda Bradshaw. Calls herself Joey."

"Got it. Take care of yourself. And, Ash?"

"Yeah?"

"Just in case she *is* our slasher, you be real careful not to let on that the amnesia is just a cover."

He disconnected and got dressed just in time. She was back at the speed of sound and, moments later, pushing him through the corridors in a wheelchair that was completely unnecessary, but required. Probably by the hospital's lawyers. She seemed nervous. Her eyes darted around, seemingly watching everyone. Ash steered himself toward the nurse's desk, taking her with him. He asked the nurse on duty for a pad and a pen and turned toward his "wife."

"What's your address?"

"Eight twenty-nine Gaskin, in Clay. Why?"

He jotted it down. "Just in case anyone tries to reach me here, I want to let them know where I am."

Her eyes widened. She reached past him to rip the top page from the notepad and then crumpled it in her fist. "I don't think that's such a good idea."

Ash got up out of the wheelchair and leaned negligently against the desk so he could see every expression that crossed her face, eye to eye. There was heightened color to her cheeks. Her full lips were parted slightly in agitation. She was one hell of an attractive woman. "Why not?" he asked.

"I just...I don't like my home address being... readily available to any nut case who happens to ask for it, that's all." She tugged the pen from his hand, leaned over the pad and wrote something down. She shoved it across the desk to the nurse. "If anyone tries to reach Mister—my husband—give them this number."

"So during my sentence, will I be allowed visitors?"

She whirled to face him, her hair flying. God, she was jumpy. He smiled so she'd know he was kidding. He wasn't, but it wouldn't pay to let too much show. His "wife's" expression eased slightly, and she picked up a large zippered bag from the desk, offered him a shaky smile, and started for the elevators.

Ash caught up within a second or two, waving off the nurse who started yelling about the mandatory wheelchair. "What've you got there, Joey?"

"What?" She thumped the down arrow repeatedly,

gaze raking the halls.

"The bag."

Her brows lifted, but she handed him the bag. "Your personal effects. The stuff they took off you when you were admitted. You know, wallet, loose change." She averted her eyes. "Wedding ring."

Oh, man, she didn't miss a trick, this phony wife of his. If there was a ring in that bag, she'd put it there, just now. And he hadn't seen a thing.

"Wouldn't want to go too long not wearing that," he muttered. "Feel naked without it."

"Are you being sarcastic or making a joke?" She searched his face, her own worried, wary. He shrugged. The doors slid open and she shot a nervous glance at the people inside. It took her a few ticks, as if she had to study each face individually before she made up her mind. About what, he had no idea. Ash caught the doors before they slid closed again.

"We're holding people up, Joey. And here comes that wheelchair Nazi nurse," he said, nodding toward the nurse pushing the ridiculous chair their way. "Something wrong?"

Shaking her head, she stepped into the elevator. She stood very close to him as the doors slid closed, he noticed. Her attitude was damned strange. Not like someone who was pulling a scam just to get him in the sack—if that was what she was up to. God knew, it wasn't necessary. He'd have obliged her in a New York minute if she'd simply asked. One time and one time only, of course. She was not his type. She was his anti-type, in fact. Qualification number one for the future Mrs. Ashville Coye was that she not be promiscuous enough to have sex on the first date. He'd prefer she not be promiscuous at all.

But looking at her, all tight fitting leather and centerfold hair, he thought she was a walking advertisement for a good time. That's why he figured he'd have known Joey Bradshaw was no wife of his, even if the amnesia had been real. It was in those bedroom eyes that seemed to look right through him, to his hidden fantasies. And it was in those luscious lips, so full and plump that they made a man want to taste them.

He scoffed at his own train of thought. Probably collagen.

The doors slid open and she was the first to step out. She gave a quick glance around the lobby, following it with one over her shoulder to be sure he was right behind her. Then she started for the exit. No less than seven male heads turned as she passed, he noted.

She didn't seem to notice, just strode purposefully across the parking lot while Ash followed. The July sun rebounded from the pavement, making the asphalt feel like an oven. There was no hint of a breeze, and the air was heavy and stifling. She stopped beside a monster-size, glistening black motorcycle. Grabbing a black helmet with an angular, tinted face shield, she pulled it over her head. When he stopped right behind her, she held out one that matched.

"You're kidding, right?"

She thumbed her visor back, tilted her head to one

side. "If I'd known you were being released today, I'd have brought the car."

"That's not what I—"

"Look, why don't you go back to that coffee shop off the lobby? I'll ride home and get the car." She frowned, and rushed on. "No, no, that won't work. Can't leave you alone." Then she she snapped her fingers. "I know, we'll call a cab and leave the bike—"

"You talk too much, you know that?" He grabbed the helmet and pulled it on, wincing as it slid past the bandaged wound on his head. The amnesia might be phony, but the damned concussion was real enough. "I'm fine. I was just wondering about you." He looked doubtfully at the bike as he fastened the strap under his chin. "Looks like a lot for a little thing like you to handle. Mind if I drive?"

"The last time you drove, you wound up in the back of an ambulance." She flipped her visor back down with a snap and swung one leg over the seat. Well, he'd managed to tweak her temper. He'd been wondering if her concern for his health and happiness would have any bounds.

The Harley was low slung despite its size. Still, her feet barely reached the pavement. She kicked the motor to life and revved it. Ash caught a whiff of gasoline and exhaust, sighed in resignation and climbed on behind her. He slid forward on the slanting seat until he was pressed to her backside. Putting his arms around her waist, he decided he might not mind the ride so much.

She caught his hands in hers and moved them until

they just rested on her sides, above her hips. Again the visor was thumbed up. She twisted her head and shouted above the roar of the motor. "Move 'em and lose 'em...darling."

He thumbed his visor back, too, and tried for a pained expression. "I'm sorry."

Her anger vanished. Her huge eyes softened and she almost pouted. "It's just less distracting this way, Ash. That's all."

He nodded, a little surprised at how easily he could skirt her anger by acting hurt. A con artist centerfold with a heart of gold. He could hardly wait to find out what she was up to.

And whether it had anything to do with the Slasher murders.

He pushed his visor down. She did likewise. A second later they lurched forward and shot into traffic.

Look for FORGOTTEN
available now.

ABOUT THE AUTHOR

New York Times bestselling author Maggie Shayne has published more than 60 novels and 23 novellas. She has written for 7 publishers and 2 soap operas, has racked up 15 Rita Award nominations and actually, finally, won the damn thing in 2005.

Maggie lives in a beautiful, century old, happily haunted farmhouse named "Serenity" in the wildest wilds of Cortland County, NY, with her husband and soul mate, Lance. They share a pair of English Mastiffs, Dozer & Daisy, and a little English Bulldog, Niblet, and the wise guardian and guru of them all, the feline Glory, who keeps the dogs firmly in their places. Maggie's a Wiccan high priestess (legal clergy even) and an avid follower of the Law of Attraction

Connect with Maggie

Maggie's Website: www.MaggieShayne.com
Wings In The Night: www.WingsInTheNight.com
Maggie's Bliss Blog: www.MaggiesBlissBlog.com
Coffee House Blog:
MaggieShayne.com/CoffeeHouse
Twitter: www.Twitter.com/MaggieShayne
Facebook:
www.Facebook.com/MaggieShayneAuthor